POSEIDON'S RANSOM

PHILIP CAINE

3

POSEIDON'S RANSOM

First paperback edition printed 2018 in the United Kingdom

ISBN 9780993374852

Published by REDOAK
www.philipcaine.com
For more copies of this book, please use the website above.

Critique & Editing: Gillian Ogilvie
Technical Editor: Malcolm Caine

Cover Design: www.gonzodesign.co.uk

Printed in Great Britain:
www.print2demand.co.uk

ABOUT THE AUTHOR

Philip's career began in hotel management and then transitioned to offshore North Sea, where he worked the boom years on Oil Rigs, Barges & Platforms. Seventeen years passed, and Philip returned to onshore projects taking a three year contract to manage accommodation bases in North & West Africa.

From Africa, Philip moved to the 'Former Soviet Union' where he directed multiple projects in Kazakhstan & Russia, a particularly exciting seven years where dealings with the KGB were an everyday event.

The end of the Iraq War in 2003 took Philip to Baghdad where, as Operations Director, he controlled the operations & management of multiple accommodation bases for the American Coalition. He left Baghdad in 2010. The last three years of his career were spent running a couple of support services companies in Dubai.

Philip's time in the Middle East has been the inspiration for his adventure thrillers, and the JACK CASTLE series.

Philip semi-retired in 2014 and began writing fiction in February 2015, after joining Ulverston Writers Group. His first novel, PICNIC IN IRAQ, is an adventure treasure hunt set in Iraq. The sequel, TO CATCH A FOX, is an exciting rescue mission set in Syria. BREAKFAST IN BEIRUT, sees the main character, Jack Castle, working for MI6 in the Middle East. His fourth novel, THE HOLLOW PRESIDENT, reveals the truth about a corrupt and murderous American President. AMERICAN RONIN tells the tale of a rogue CIA agents working for the North Koreans.

POSEIDON'S RANSOM is his sixth book in the JACK CASTLE series.

5

A country will pay anything to safeguard its people…
and then do everything possible to get it back…

Anon.

POSEIDON'S RANSOM

Prologue

Autumn 2013
'The Philippines'

It felt as though his face was on fire. The pain was unbelievable. The surgeon, reputedly the best in the Far East, had explained the procedures and outlined the issues during the post-op period. But Greg Stoneham had not expected anything as painful as this. The morphine helped a lot. But he was concerned he may become dependent and chose to bear the pain as much as possible, taking short periods of relief with the effective opiate.

The clinic in Manilla was expensive, in fact probably the most expensive in the world. The one-and-a-half million dollar procedure he'd selected was full facial reconstruction. Drastic, costly, but necessary. The alternative was to spend the rest of his life living in the shadows. Not an option. Greg Stoneham, rogue CIA agent, now contract terrorist, had to disappear.

A team of three surgeons had taken slivers of bone from his pelvis and laminated his cheekbones. The same procedure altered his jawline and chin. The insertion of small pellets of gel, changed the look of his eyebrows, and his broken nose had been straightened and rebuilt. The scar across his head was removed and the old leg injury, sustained in a helicopter crash in Panama, had been corrected. The leg, now in ankle-to-thigh plaster, would not have a limp.

His head and shoulders were encased in a state-of-the-art cocoon, giving total protection against infection during the critical forty-eight-hour post-op period. Full recuperation would last seven to eight weeks, during which time a complete hair transplant would be done.

As the pain level in his face increased, Stoneham pressed the button to release the welcome hit of morphine. The nurse at his bedside stood up and checked the various drips running into his arms. As she sat down she thought she saw her patient smile.

He pressed the button again. The pain in his face subsided to a dull ache, as his thoughts flashed to the future. *Greg Stoneham is gone. There is no Stoneham. In a few weeks' time Mr Rick Washington will take his place.*

Chapter One
Summer 2014
'Greek Gods'

In Greek mythology, Kronos was the leader of the first generation of Titans, the divine descendants of Uranus, the sky, and Gaia, the earth. He overthrew his father and ruled during the mythological Golden Age, until he too was overthrown by his own sons, Poseidon, Hades and Zeus. The three brother Gods then became the overall rulers and held absolute power within the Cosmos.

Poseidon, Hades and Zeus were now the names given to the latest generation of 'Olympus Class' nuclear submarines serving in Her Majesty's Royal Navy. These three ships, usually referred to as 'boats' within the service, are the most powerful and sophisticated ever built, each with a cost well in excess of three and a half billion pounds.

After construction at the Barrow-in-Furness shipyard, in the North West of England, each submarine deploys to the Royal Naval Base at Faslane, Scotland. It is here the boats are stocked and armed with their payload of Trident nuclear missiles, cruise missiles and hi-ex torpedoes, thereby becoming the UK's first and last line of defence.

* * *

In Whitehall the summer sun streamed in through the big windows transforming the austere office. The ancient oak panelling reflected the rays and brightened not only the room, but the occupant's demeanour. Sir Anthony Grainger, the Secretary of State for Defence, sipped from the steaming cup of Earl Grey as he read through the security brief outlining his planned visit, and short voyage, to and on, HMS Poseidon.

The beep of his smartphone broke his concentration. He looked at the screen, OLIVIA CALLING. He put down the document and swiped the screen. 'Hello, darling?'

'Anthony,' her voice trembled, clearly upset and sobbing.

Grainger stood up. 'Olivia? What on earth is wrong, darling?'

'Sir Anthony.' It was a man's voice. Quiet, calm, American, 'Please listen carefully.'

'Who the hell is this?' The line was silent for several seconds . . . 'Hello? Hello?'

'Sir Anthony. Please stay calm and listen carefully. If you do as we instruct, your family will be safe.'

'What do you mean? What do you want?'

'Sir Anthony, we have your wife and daughter. If you want to see them both alive again, you will do exactly as you are instructed.'

Grainger's voice was shaky. 'Yes, yes anything.'

'You will not contact the security services or confide in anyone.'

'Yes, I . . .'

'Please, Sir Anthony, just listen. You will be given instructions later today. In the meantime, please go about your duties as usual. And, Sir Anthony, please be assured, we will kill your family if you deviate in any way from our instructions.'

'Yes, I mean no.' He couldn't control the panic in his voice, 'Yes whatever you want. Please. Can I speak to my wife?'

The line went silent.

Chapter Two
'Stay Calm'

Summers in the West of Scotland are short lived and generally far cooler than the rest of the country. The stiff breeze coming off the waters of Gare Loch chilled the air and the gathering clouds heralded another wet day.

HMS Poseidon rested at its mooring in the Faslane Naval Base. The watery sunlight, glinting on the sleek black hull gave off a benign appearance that belied the true capability of this deadly war machine.

The jeep came to a stop a few yards from the gangway. The two Naval Police came smartly to attention and snapped a salute as the officer stepped out of the vehicle. Returning the salute, the officer walked onto the gangway as his smartphone beeped.

In his cabin, Commander Gordon Dowling fought to stay calm. He'd been in many stressful situations throughout his career and always managed to control his emotions and respond professionally. He was known for his cool and calm leadership. But this was different. This was personal. This was his family. The call on the gangway had shocked him, the voice of the American, speaking matter-of-factly about killing his wife and sons.

'Stay calm and act normally, Commander,' he'd been told.

The knock on the door broke into his thoughts. He cleared his throat and said, 'Come.'

The door slid open and Stephen Pike, the First Officer entered. Pike's face was solemn. He closed the door and said, 'Is this for real?'

Dowling and Pike had served together for the last three years but had known each other for more than fifteen. They were not only colleagues, but close friends.

'Take a seat, Steve.' Dowling went to the small fridge and took out two bottles of water. Handing one to Pike, he said, 'What did they tell you?'

Pike's face looked drained. He ran his hand over his bald head and exhaled deeply. 'They have my mother and father . . . To do as instructed . . . Not to call the police. To come and speak to you.'

Dowling swallowed half the contents of the bottle, then fiddled with the cap as he looked at his second in command. 'They have Kathy and my boys. They said they'd kill them if I didn't comply with instructions.'

Pike leaned back in the small chair, 'And what were they?'

'To do nothing and wait until you came to me. Further instructions would follow. For a split second I thought you had something to do with this.'

'Are you serious, Gordon?'

The shocked look on the First Officer's face brought a, 'Sorry, Steve,' from Dowling, 'Christ, what the hell d' these bastards want?'

Chapter Three
'The Farmhouse'

The view from the front of the old Welsh farmhouse looked down the valley and out to the Irish Sea. The building had been abandoned for almost a year, but was still in good condition, weatherproof and, more importantly for Rick Washington, remote. The evening wind was chill, and he pulled the collar of his coat up around his neck. He watched the small van as it wound its way up the side of the hill, the road winding back and forth to accommodate the incline.

He hunched his shoulders against the wind, *Fucking England was cold enough, but Wales! And this was supposed to be summer*, he thought. Washington had spent the last year in the Philippines and his bones were definitely not used to this Welsh climate.

The reconstructive surgery he'd undergone in Manilla had totally changed his appearance, and he doubted his own mother would recognise him now. The implanted full head of thick black hair played to his vanity and the absence of the painful limp was a blessing.

For a second his thoughts flashed to the small ranch in Panama. The old goatherd who'd saved Greg Stoneham from the helicopter crash, and the beautiful girl who'd tended his injuries. She'd fixed him up pretty good, but the leg had not been set well. *Consuela Sanchez,* he thought, *you saved my life honey. But you wouldn't know me now. You wouldn't know Rick Washington.*

The van was still struggling up the side of the hill as the evening rain began to fall. A voice from behind pulled his thoughts back from Panama. 'They here yet, boss?'

Washington didn't turn around. 'A few minutes. You ready for them?'

'Yes, boss.'

'Then get-the-fuck back in there.'

A few minutes later the van pulled into the ramshackle farmyard. Washington waved to the two men as they stepped out of the cab. 'How'd it go?' he said.

The men walked over and nodded. 'No problems, boss. All good.'

'Okay, let's get 'em inside. This summer weather is freezing my balls off.'

They walked over to the van and, before opening the rear doors, the three pulled on full-face balaclavas.

The old man and woman were roughly pulled from the rear of the van. 'Take it easy,' snarled Washington to his men, 'no need for that.' He stood in front of the couple and said, 'Mr and Mrs Pike, I know you are scared, but you'll have nothing to fear if you do as you are told. You will not be harmed. You see we are wearing masks. If we intended to kill you, we would not worry about you seeing our faces. But do not doubt us. If you do not comply with every instruction you will be killed.'

The woman began to sob and the man put his arms around her pulling her close.

'Okay, get inside,' snapped one of the henchmen, then, after seeing the scathing look from Washington, continued, 'Please.'

The inside of the farmhouse was basic, but after Washington's men had cleaned-up the place and got the portable generator running, would be comfortable enough for the next few days.

A small hallway opened into a large central lounge. The Pikes were ushered through the big room and up the stairs. Several doors ran off the landing, one of which stood open. The three masked men accompanied them to the room. The one with the American voice said, 'Please make yourselves comfortable.' He walked over to a thin rope next to the door. 'If you need the bathroom, or if you're ill, please pull this and one of my men will come. I believe you have your medication, Mrs Pike, and I understand that will be sufficient for the next few days. We don't expect to be here longer than three or four at the most. There will be hot food in about an hour. Now if you will excuse me.'

'Why are you doing this, sir?' said Mr Pike.

'I'm afraid I cannot answer any questions. Please just stay calm and try and relax. This will all be over in a few days.'

The American and the two men left the room. The door was closed, followed by the sound of the lock being turned.

Joan Pike had stopped sobbing and looked around the room. There were two inflatable beds with a pile of new sheets and duvets, still in the wrappings, on each. On the table in the corner was a case of water, teabags, coffee and biscuits, some cartons of milk and a kettle.

George Pike looked at his wife. 'Looks like we have three-star accommodation, dear.' He went to the single window and found it to be screwed shut and the panes covered with white paint. He turned to see Joan, who now sat in one of the shabby armchairs. 'How're you feeling, old girl?'

She looked at her husband and took in a deep breath. 'Confused, angry and afraid.'

'Well, in that case there's only one thing to do, my dear.'

'Oh . . . And what might that be, George?'

'I'll put the kettle on.'

In the adjacent bedroom, Kathy Dowling and her two sons had similar accommodation to the Pikes. In the third room, Lady Olivia Grainger and her daughter Caroline stood in silence, their ears pressed hard to the old oak door, and listened to the goings-on across the landing.

Chapter Four
'Hugo Boss'

In his Knightsbridge pied-a-terre, Sir Anthony Grainger stood at the window and looked out over the small park. The Ormolu mantel clock softly chimed 4am. He had not slept. He hadn't eaten, and the pain in his head was getting worse. He went to the bathroom and took some Paracetamol from the cabinet. Returning to the drawing room he poured a small amount of scotch into a crystal tumbler, raised it to his lips, then stopped. *No alcohol, need a clear head. Stay calm. Whatever needs to be done,* he thought. He picked up a small bottle of sparkling water, cracked the cap, and then washed the pills down. He went to the window again and watched as a taxi dropped off a fare, a couple of houses down the street. He looked up to the big full moon, and said, 'Please, God. Please protect my girls.'

The sleek black Jaguar pulled up to the curb at six-o'clock. The driver and Special Branch officer were both surprised to see Sir Anthony, uncharacteristically, waiting at the top of the steps. Both men quickly exited the vehicle and, as the driver held open the rear door, the protection officer trotted up the steps, and said, 'Good morning, Sir Anthony,'
'Morning.'
The officer frowned slightly at the unexpected curtness, then picked up the small holdall. 'Everything alright, sir?'

No reply from Grainger, who walked swiftly down to the waiting car. The driver smiled and said, 'Good morning, sir,' as Grainger climbed in.

The officer dropped the bag into the boot, then looked at the driver, who shrugged. It was clear the Secretary of State was not his usual friendly self today.

The Times newspaper, on the seat next to Grainger, had been left unopened and the crossword, which was usually completed before he arrived at his office, was not attempted. At that hour the drive, from Knightsbridge to London City Heliport, had been reasonably swift and the Jaguar pulled up to the VIP entrance a little after six-thirty.

A security guard came out of the booth and checked the driver's I.D. Glancing in the back; he recognised Sir Anthony and quickly stepped back. He turned and nodded to his colleague and the heavy electronic gate hissed open. As the Jaguar passed through the guard gave a cursory salute, then watched as the big car drove away.

A couple of minutes later the vehicle pulled up to the rear of the terminal building. Another security guard stepped forward, as the driver quickly got out and flashed his I.D. The guard nodded and stepped back. Sir Anthony, his face solemn, climbed out, as his protection officer collected the bag from the boot.

Grainger held out his hand and said, 'I'll take it from here, Gary.'

'Sir?' said the officer.

'I won't need you anymore today. Thank you, Gary.'

'With respect sir, that's against protocol.'

'I'll be fine, Gary. I'm in the helicopter from here all the way to the naval base.'

'But, sir . . . '

Grainger took his holdall, and with a stern look on his face said, 'I shall see you back here in a couple of days.'

After watching their charge disappear into the terminal, the two Special Branch officers climbed back into the big Jag. 'What the fuck was that all about?' said Gary.

The First Class Lounge was quiet, with only a dozen or so people sitting around reading papers, or eating breakfast. A young female attendant recognised him and said, 'Good morning, Sir Anthony. May I get you anything, sir?'

Grainger, who'd normally have been the epitome of charm, dismissed the girl with a simple, 'No thank you.'

The girl smiled and walked away, as Grainger scanned the room. His attention landed on two men in the far corner, neither of whom were reading or eating. The older of the two stood and nodded slightly. Grainger joined the men and sat down. No handshakes were offered.

'Sir Anthony, good morning. I'm Frank Baine.' Grainger noted the hint of a German accent. 'And this is my colleague, Ravinda Patel. He's our resident . . . err, what's the expression, computer geek.'

Grainger nodded, but said nothing. Baine was well-built and in his mid-fifties. Patel was younger, maybe 28 or 30, clearly Asian, with rimless glasses that perched on the end of his hawkish nose. Both wore expensive three piece suits. *Hugo Boss,* thought Grainger, but neither looked comfortable in them.

'As you've been advised, we'll be accompanying you on your trip, Sir Anthony,' said Baine.

Grainger looked solemn. 'Yes, I was told. How are my wife and daughter?'

Baine smiled and said softly, 'They are both safe and in good health. Have no fear, sir.'

The young attendant came to the table. 'Excuse me, gentlemen. May I get you anything?'

The two men shook their heads. Grainger looked at the girl and said, 'Just water, please.'

Over half an hour passed with no conversation, then at seven-fifteen, a smartly uniformed man came to the table. 'Excuse me, Sir Anthony. Your aircraft is ready for boarding. If you'd come with me please.'

The three stood, each picked up their bags, and followed the attendant from the lounge and down to a waiting minibus. A few moments later they pulled up alongside a Naval Jet Ranger helicopter. With their bags stowed and his passengers strapped in, the pilot turned and said, 'Good morning, gentlemen. Weather is good all the way to Scotland, so we should have wheels down at the base, in one hour 'n fifty minutes. Please relax and enjoy the flight.'

The engine whined into life and the aircraft shook slightly as the rotors increased speed. As the tail rose, the pilot twisted the throttle and the helicopter climbed into the clear morning sky.

Baine took out his smartphone and opened the Messenger application. Sir Anthony watched as the big man tapped away at the screen.

In the Welsh farmhouse, Rick Washington responded to the beep from his phone. He swiped the screen, then smiled as he read the message. CONTACT MADE. AIRBORNE.

Chapter Five
'Three, Not Two'

It was a little before nine-thirty when the Jet Ranger began it's decent onto the helipad at the Faslane Naval Base. A Royal Navy jeep was waiting and, as the chopper's engine shut down and the rotors came to a stop, two naval security officers climbed out.

Grainger, Baine and Patel walked over to the jeep, as the heli-guard unloaded their bags and carried them to the vehicle.

'Sir Anthony. Good morning,' said one of the officers, a puzzled look on his face. 'We were advised there would only be two in your party, sir.'

'That's correct, these are my two colleagues,' said the minister.

'No, sorry, sir,' continued the officer apologetically, 'I was advised it would be yourself and one other. A special branch officer.'

'Then you were advised incorrectly, young man. Now can we please move along?'

The officer smiled. 'Err . . . yes, sir. Sorry, sir,' then stepped aside, as Grainger climbed into the back of the jeep, quickly followed by the other two men.

It took almost ten minutes to drive from the helipad to the sea-ward side of the base. The jeep drove in amongst warehouses, workshops and office buildings, eventually arriving at the dock area. They drove along the quayside and, after passing several navy ships, finally pulled up at a formidable set of security gates. Two heavily armed security officers approached the vehicle and as one checked I.D. the other walked around the jeep. The same question was raised with regards to the number of individuals in the Secretary of State's party and, after stringent intervention from Grainger, the gates were finally opened and the jeep allowed through.

The vehicle continued for a few hundred yards along the quayside, the huge expanse of water that is Gare Loch to the left, and finally came to a stop alongside Britain's latest nuclear submarine, HMS Poseidon.

It was clear Sir Anthony's arrival had been passed to the sub, as there were six smartly uniformed submariners standing in line and to attention, along the bow of the vessel. The Commander and First Officer stood on the quayside, waiting for the minister.

As the jeep came to a stop, the two naval officers snapped smartly to attention and saluted. Grainger and his two companions exited the vehicle. 'Good morning, gentlemen,' said Grainger, as he offered his hand.

Dowling shook hands and said, 'Good morning, Sir Anthony. Welcome aboard HMS Poseidon, sir. I'm Commander Dowling, and this is my First Officer, Stephen Pike.'

Grainger shook hands with the officer and then said, matter-of-factly, 'This is Mr Baine and Mr Patel; they'll be joining us today.'

Commander Dowling looked at the two men. No handshake was offered. 'Let's get aboard, shall we, sir?'

A few minutes later the five were seated in the small officer's mess. Sir Anthony, a stern look on his face turned to Baine and said, 'You have our families. I have got you on board. Now, will you tell us what the hell it is you want?'

Baine looked at the faces of the three men now under his control. 'All in good time, Sir Anthony, all in good time,' then turning to Dowling continued, 'what time do we set sail, Commander?'

'We are due to depart on the midday tide. But we aren't going anywhere until I, we, know our families are safe.'

'Commander, you are in no position to ask questions.' The big man smiled. 'As you've been advised, your families are safe and will be released when our demands are complied with.'

'And what are your demands?' said Grainger.

'Oh, we'll get to that. As soon as we are out at sea, Sir Anthony. Now if Mr Patel and I could see our accommodation, please?'

The small room was silent for several seconds. Dowling turned to his First Officer. 'Steve. Can you show these, gentlemen,' the word was said with obvious distaste, 'to their cabin please?'

After the three had left, Dowling said, 'What the hell is going on, Sir Anthony?'

The minister leaned back in his seat and sucked in a deep breath. 'May I have some water please, Commander?'

'Yes, sir, of course.' The officer went to a small fridge, removed a bottle and poured half the contents

27

into a glass. 'Sir,' he said, as he placed the glass on the table. 'Are you okay. You don't look well, sir.'

Grainger took a small silver box from his waistcoat pocket, removed a couple of tiny pills and washed them down with the water. 'I'll be fine . . . Need to deal with this situation. I'll be fine. Thank you, Commander.'

'Can I get you anything else, sir? Should I get a medic?'

'No, I'm fine, Commander. Really. Thank you.'

Dowling took his seat and said, 'Any idea who the hell these people are, sir?'

Grainger sucked in another deep breath. 'Terrorists . . . and we have just given them access to the most powerful warship this country owns.'

Chapter Six
'Underway'

At eleven-thirty, the sound of the engines being fired up caused Frank Baine to rise from his bunk. Patel was working on his laptop. 'Sounds like we're about to get underway,' said Baine.

Patel turned and smiled. 'Good, the sooner we're out at sea, the safer we'll be.'

Baine stood up and stretched the muscles in his back. 'Right, let's go find Grainger and the Captain.'

Patel put the laptop back in its case. Baine picked up his bag, 'Okay, Rav, let's go to work.'

They left the cabin and stepped out into the companionway. Baine stopped the first submariner he saw and said, 'Excuse me. Could you help us find the Captain, please?'

The young sailor stood up straight. 'Yes, sir. Please follow me. Oh, and it's Commander, not Captain, sir.'

Baine smiled. 'Yes, yes, of course, Commander Dowling,' then under his breath said, 'whatever.'

'He'll be on the tower, sir, we're about to cast-off.'

The two hijackers followed the young seaman through the vessel. Each area they passed through was busy with officers and men going about their duty, in preparation for departure. They eventually arrived at the main control room, just as the First Officer was about to ascend the ladder to the conning-tower. The young seaman saluted and said, 'Sir. These gentlemen are looking for the Commander.'

Pike returned the salute and said, 'Thank you. I'll see to them. Dismissed.'

The control room was as busy as the other areas. A dozen or more seamen, of various ranks, worked away monitoring screens and systems in preparation for sea. Pike noticed the two hijackers were taking in the scene before them. There was an almost unperceivable nod between Baine and Patel, then the big man said, 'Very impressive, Mr Pike.'

The First Officer looked Baine straight in the eyes, then pointed upwards. 'The Commander is on deck. You can leave your bags here.'

Baine gave a sickly smile. 'We'll hang on to them,' he said, then nodded to the ladder, 'after you, Mr Pike.'

The three climbed the ladder in turn and came out at the top of the conning-tower. Commander Dowling, along with two other seamen, was supervising the manoeuvre from the quayside. Sir Anthony Grainger was also there. All wore hooded weatherproofs; protection against the rising wind and falling rain. No offer of coats was extended to Baine and Patel, who looked somewhat foolish standing in nothing more than designer suits.

Dowling nodded to his First Officer, as Pike emerged from the hatch. Then, into a hand-held radio, Dowling said, 'Clear stern-lines.'

A voice from the radio confirmed the order. 'Clear stern-lines, aye, sir.'

A few moments later all lines securing the warship, were released and pulled from the water. The engines increased in volume in response to Dowling's command, 'Starboard thrusters to ten percent.'

As HMS Poseidon moved slowly away from the sea-wall, Grainger watched Baine tap out a message on his smartphone.

In the old Welsh farmhouse, Rick Washington smiled as he read the message. UNDERWAY.

Chapter Seven
'Exceptional Thieves'

It took a little over an hour for HMS Poseidon to sail from its Faslane Base, down the length of Gare Loch and out through the Firth of Clyde, into the Irish Sea. Another hour saw the vessel off the coast of Northern Ireland.

Soon after the boat had departed, Baine had called Grainger and the two officers into the small mess room. After the room had been cleared of catering staff, Baine stood up and smiled his sickly smile, then began in a quiet voice. 'Now, gentlemen. You've all done well to this point. Your families are safe and will, as we have promised, remain so, as long as you co-operate.'

'Get to the point. What the hell d'you want?' said a stern-faced Commander Dowling.

There was no mistaking the tension in the room. The big man continued and the smile disappeared. 'Yes, thank you, Commander. I'm coming to that.' Baines eyes narrowed. He stepped back from the table and unbuttoned his shirt. This time Patel had the smile, when he saw the look on the faces of Grainger and the two officers.

'What the hell is that?' said the minister.

Around Baine's waist was, what looked like, a normal light canvas money belt. Three small pockets were secured with Velcro. All eyes in the room were on the belt as Baine carefully opened one of the pockets. The only sound was the noise of the Velcro fasteners being pulled apart. Gently he removed a small glass vial, about the size of a man's thumb. The overhead lighting sparkled benignly on the glass as Baine held it, almost reverently, between his fingers.

'Oh, my God. What is that,' said a pale-faced Grainger.

Baine looked at the faces of the men in front of him, and then turned his gaze on the glass container. 'This, Mr Secretary of Defence, is one hundred grams of Ricin. And I have two more like this.' Baine pointed to the belt around his waist.

'Oh, God,' said Grainger again.

'I'm sure you all know what this can do, but just in case you don't, I'll explain. Ricin may be ingested or inhaled and the slightest amount, the slightest miniscule amount, is capable of killing a man within a few hours. If these vials are broken,' he turned the container carefully around in his fingers, 'and the spores enter the atmosphere, they will pass through this vessel's air-conditioning system in seconds and infect every person on-board.'

'Including you,' said the First Officer.

'Yes, including me . . . but I'm being paid a very large amount of money to take that risk, Mr Pike. But hopefully it won't come to that.'

'Paid?' said Dowling, 'What the hell kind of terrorist are you?'

The sickly smile returned to the big man's face. 'Who said we were terrorists?'

'So, not terrorists?' said Dowling, 'hijackers then?'

Baine frowned. 'What need is there for titles? Let's just say we're businessmen, negotiating the return of this very expensive submarine, for an equally large amount of money.'

'Money? So, you're just common thieves?' said Grainger.

Baine's frown deepened. 'Common? Oh no, Sir Anthony, I think we are exceptional thieves.'

Patel stood up and said, 'I need to get started.'

Baine returned the vial carefully to the belt, then fastened up his shirt. 'Yes of course. Now, Mr Pike. Would you be kind enough to show Ravinda here, to Weapons Control, please?'

Both officers stood up. This time it was Commander Dowling's turn to smirk. 'That will do you no good. There's no way you can get control of any of our weapons. Even we can't do that, unless we are sent pre-arranged launch-codes. Our missiles are totally useless without those codes.'

Baine smiled and placed his hand on Ravinda Patel's shoulder. 'My young friend here is one of the top computer programmers in the world. In fact you may have heard of one or two of his more audacious hacks?'

The little Asian grinned as Baine continued.

'I'm sure you've heard of the cyber-attack on America's NORAD weapons system a couple of years ago? And then last year, when the Singapore Stock Exchange crashed, wiping billions from the Asian markets?'

Patel beamed as the big man extolled the young Indian's capabilities.

Baine's smile disappeared, and he turned to the First Officer. 'Now. Will you please escort Ravinda to the Weapons Control Room, Mr Pike?'

After the two men left, Grainger said, 'And what happens now?'

Baine's sickly smile was back. He looked at his watch, and said, 'As we speak, contact is being made with the British Government.'

'Contact?' said Dowling.

'Yes, Commander. The return of this warship, the non-release of nuclear missiles, the safety of your crew, and of course the release of your own families, has a very high price.'

Dowling shook his head slightly. 'And what price is that?'

Baine sat back in his chair, the smile widened. 'Three billion pounds, Commander.'

Chapter Eight
'Downing Street'

The rain in Wales had persisted all night, but the morning brought clear blue skies and a pale sunshine. Rick Washington was in the small room at the back of the old farmhouse. Equipment had been set up to monitor hidden closed-circuit cameras on the property and the surrounding countryside. If anyone approached the location, he would know well in advance.

One of Washington's men was working on a laptop. He turned and said, 'Okay, boss, that's the voice-scrambler and cloaking device set up. You can call anyone, anywhere. They won't be able to recognise your voice, or identify this location.'

'Good,' said Washington, as he patted the man's back, 'good job.' He looked at his watch and smiled. 'Time to make a phone-call then.'

* * *

In her Downing Street office, the Prime Minister listened in disbelief, as the Home Secretary spoke.

'Three billion pounds?' said the PM.

'Yes, ma'am.'

'Do we know if this threat is viable? Have we been in contact with Poseidon?'

'Yes, ma'am. We made contact with the submarine as soon as the call came in. There are two terrorists on-board.'

'Two? Only two? How on God's earth did two people manage to get on-board and take over a submarine with a crew of what, a hundred and fifty?'

The Home Secretary cleared his throat. 'They were with the Secretary of Defence, ma'am.'

'Sir Anthony Grainger took them on-board!'

'Yes, Prime Minister. We believe he was coerced. His family were kidnapped.'

'Have we verified that?'

'Yes, ma'am. Poseidon's Commander and First Officer's families are also missing.'

'Good God.'

'We have Special Branch and MI6 making enquiries, ma'am. We hope we can find the families.'

'Yes, yes, of course. But what about the weapons? Please tell me they cannot release any missiles.'

The Home Secretary looked sheepish. 'We're told they've managed to hack-into the weapons system and circumvent the launch-codes.'

The PM leaned forward, elbows on her desk, head in her hands. 'Oh, my God.'

'Ma'am we . . .'

The Prime Minister looked up and raised her hand. 'Right, call all relevant ministers and military, for an immediate COBRA meeting. I want everyone here in one hour.'

'Yes, ma'am.'

The Home Secretary stood up and was about to leave, when the PM said, 'And you'd better get the Governor of the Bank of England here too.'

'Very well, ma'am.'

'And, Home Secretary.'

'Ma'am?'

'Total media blackout. We do not want any panic.'

After the door closed, the PM pressed the intercom, and said, 'Gordon, please get me the American President, on the secure line.

The atmosphere in the room at the back of number 10, was clearly tense. Several ministers and high ranking military officers stood around chatting. The smell of fresh coffee permeated the air.

Fifty seven minutes after the Home Secretary had put out the call to the government hierarchy, the Prime Minister entered. 'Good morning everyone. Thank you for coming so quickly.'

Cups were discarded onto various side tables, as the members of the COBRA committee took their seats.

Unlike number 10's main Cabinet Office, with its large mahogany table and elegant Georgian windows, Cabinet Office, Briefing Room A, which gives its name to the sinister acronym COBRA, is a modern communications centre. Windowless, and with its concealed lighting, large screen wall-mounted monitors and contemporary furniture, it is more suited to a James Bond movie than a British Government office.

'Home Secretary,' said the PM, as she opened the leather bound folder in front of her.

'Thank you, ma'am.' The Home Secretary leaned forward and looked around the table. 'Ladies and gentlemen, if you would please open your folders. The short brief in front of you summarises the current situation.'

Admiral Sir Horatio Staines, The Chief of the Defence Staff was the first to speak. 'This is not possible. We've considered this scenario and no way could a band of terrorists take over one of our submarines. We . . .'

The withering look from the PM caused the admiral to stop in mid-sentence. He cleared his throat. 'Excuse me, ma'am.'

'Yes, Admiral. Up until ninety minutes ago, I would have agreed with you. But it's clear the unthinkable is taking place. Our purpose this morning is to decide, in,' she looked at her watch, 'five hours and fifty four minutes, to pay Poseidon's ransom or destroy a multi-billion pound submarine, with one hundred and fifty of our service personnel on board.'

The COBRA meeting had gone on for over three hours. Now back in her office the Prime Minister looked gaunt and strained. At her desk, she opened a drawer and took out a small bottle of Paracetamols. She washed three of the capsules down with strong coffee, then pressed the intercom.

'Yes, ma'am,' said her PA.

'Graham, please ask the Governor to come in now.'

A few seconds later the knock on the door was met with a, 'Come,' from the PM.

The door was held open by her PA, as the smartly dressed man entered. 'Anything else, ma'am?'

'That's all for now, Graham. Thank you.' She stood and gestured to a fine leather chair in front of the big desk. 'Governor, sorry to keep you waiting so long. Please have a seat.'

'Not at all, Prime Minister. I'm at your disposal.'

The PM frowned slightly. 'Yes, quite. We have an extremely serious and critical situation, which is unfolding as we speak.'

'Anything I can do to help, you only have to ask, ma'am.'

She frowned again at the interruption and continued. 'We may need to move a large amount of money, at very short notice. Is that possible?'

The man nodded sagely. 'How much and to where, Prime Minister?'

'Three billion pounds. To a numbered account, which I'm advised is possibly in Montenegro.'

'Yes, ma'am, we can certainly do that without too much trouble. And the purpose of the transfer?'

She took a sip of the now cold coffee, and said, 'National security.'

Chapter Nine
'Tensions'

The picturesque town of Oban is situated on the West coast of Scotland. With its resident population of less than 10,000, it is normally a sleepy highland location, but in the summer the population increases, thanks to the tourists, to more than 25,000. Most of the visitors come for the scenery, some for the offshore fishing and many for the excellent golf in the area.

The sight of a helicopter landing at the Craiglarich Golf Club is not unusual, nor does it get much attention from the members and visitors, and only occasionally solicits the comment, 'Och, here we go again, anither rich bunch up frae Glasgow.'

On this occasion, it was strange to see only one person exit the clattering aircraft. After securing the chopper its pilot made his way into the Professional's Shop.

'G'mornin, sir,' said the young man behind the counter,' 'How can'a help ye?'

'Good morning,' said the pilot. 'I'm here to pick up some visitors who'll be arriving in a couple of hours. We made arrangements to land the helicopter here.'

'Aye, sir. We were expectin ye. Ye can wait in the clubhoos.'

The pilot smiled. 'Okay. Thank you.' As he left the shop, he took out his smartphone and tapped out two words. In the old Welsh farmhouse, Rick Washington's phone beeped. He swiped the screen and smiled at the message. IN OBAN.

In Downing Street the situation was now critical. Reports had been passed, via the Home Secretary, to the PM, none of which were good. Neither the police, Special Branch, or MI5 had made any progress with finding the kidnapped families. There had been some reports from the odd neighbour of 'goings-on' during the previous nights, but no one could help with much more than a few sketchy details.

The deadline was fast approaching, and tensions were high.

In the White House, the President was meeting with his security council. The Chief of Naval Operations, Admiral Kelsey Morgan was speaking. 'Our ballistic submarine USS Jackson is on station, south of Iceland, Mister President. It can be brought into play immediately you give the order, sir. We can take out Poseidon with a cruise missile before they knew what hit them. Just give the order.'

The President looked at the man sitting across from him. The slightest of frowns wrinkled his brow. 'Let's hope it won't come to that, Admiral.'

In his office in the Bank of England, the Governor waited in silence. His deputy stood at the window looking out over Threadneedle Street. The three billion pound transaction had been processed and was ready to be actioned. All that was needed was to press SEND on the computer. The sharp ring of the telephone broke the silence.

'Yes?' said the Governor. 'I understand . . . Thank you, Home Secretary.' He hung up the phone and turned to his deputy. 'Send it.'

Chapter Ten
'Craigellachie'

The weather in Wales had brightened up and sunshine streamed in through the dusty windows of the old building. The farmhouse was warm, and the front door was open to offer some airflow. Rick Washington had come outside and was sitting quietly on an old bench, engrossed in the spectacle of a peregrine falcon as it swooped to capture a small mouse or vole. He smiled as the sleek bird took off, the tiny doomed creature still wriggling in its claws.

'The perfect hunter,' he said quietly.

'Boss?' said the man as he came out of the house.

Washington didn't take his eyes of the falcon, as it rose majestically into the clear morning sky. 'Nothing,' he said.

'There's a call for you, boss.'

The American stood and for a few seconds continued to watch the bird as it disappeared into the distance, then turned to the man, put his hand on his shoulder, and said, 'Let's hope its good news, eh?'

The other men stood as Washington entered the house. 'Is this it, boss?' said one.

'We'll soon find out,' answered Washington with a wink.

In the back communications room, another of his men held the phone-handset; he too stood as the American came in. Washington took the phone and said, 'Hello?'

'Mr Boston?' the accent was East European.

'Yes,' said Washington, 'this is Mr Boston.'

'Thank you, sir. I just need to confirm your security code, please.'

'Go ahead.'

The man at the other end of the line cleared his throat. 'Red Pisces.'

'Blue Taurus,' said Washington.

The throat was cleared again. 'White Leo.'

'Black Libra,' answered the American.

'Thank you, Mr Boston, that is all correct. I can now tell you, sir, your expected transaction has been received.'

Washington smiled. 'Three billion pounds sterling?'

'That's correct, sir. We have now prepared the onward transactions to your advised accounts. We just need one final security code to expedite those transfers.'

'Okay, go ahead.'

Again, the voice was cleared. 'Horoscope.'

'Future,' said Washington.

'Thank you, sir. Please hold the line.'

Several seconds past . . . He could feel his palm on the handset was wet with sweat . . . Then the voice was back. 'Thank you for holding, Mr Boston. All the transfers have now gone through, sir. Less of course our three million dollars commission.'

'Of course, Thank you,' said the American.

'Thank you, sir. Have a wonderful day.'

Rick Washington put the phone down and stood in silence for several seconds, enjoying the moment.

'Well? What's the deal boss?'

Washington frowned at the crude interruption to his reverie, then turned and walked back into the big room. His men all stood. Expectant. Anxious. 'Well?' said one.

The American smiled. 'I hope you guys know which islands you want to buy?'

'Yes!' The roar went up.

The men danced and hugged each other, yelling, shouting. The noise clearly heard by the frightened people locked in the upstairs rooms.

Washington waited and allowed the men to enjoy their moment. Then he raised his hands and said, 'Okay gentlemen let's get ready to get the hell outta this goddam shithole. But first I have a special something for you all.' He went to a bag in the corner of the room and took out a bottle. 'Get some glasses,' he said

Five tumblers of different sizes were placed on the old table. The American poured out the amber liquid into four of them.

'You not drinking, boss?'

'Not for me, guys. I gave it up 20 years ago. But this,' he held up the bottle, 'is a 31 year old Craigellachie single malt whisky. Rumour has it Queen Elizabeth drinks this at Balmoral. And as you are now as rich as she is, I though you should try it.'

'Fucking A,' yelled one.

'Cheers your Majesty,' shouted another.

'Here's to you, boss,' said a third, as he raised his glass in salute.

They all went quiet, then raised their glasses. 'Yeah . . . Here's to you, boss. Cheers.'

It was the communication man who fell first. His eyes rolled up and his legs went from under him. A crimson spurt of blood shot across the wooden floor, as his head smashed against the old table. The others looked-on in surprise, as the blood oozed from the gash in the man's forehead. Two others, almost in unison, sank to their knees; one landing on top of the now dead communications man. The other collapsing back into the rocking chair he'd frequented these last few days. The forth, and biggest, struggled to stay upright. His look of disbelief quickly turned to anger. Washington stepped back, as the big man lurched towards him. 'Bastar . . .' The word was cut-short, as the big man's heart stopped.

For several seconds the American looked at the scene before him. He carefully replaced the cap on the deadly bottle of scotch and placed it on the old table. He turned and went out into the sunshine, took out his smartphone, and tapped out a single word.

In the bar of the Craiglarich Golf Club, the pilot was halfway through a sandwich when his phone beeped. He swiped the screen and smiled as he read the message. RENDEZVOUS.

Chapter Eleven
'Buy Kerala'

Once Ravinda Patel had secured access to Poseidon's weapons system, there had been little else to do but wait. On Baine's instructions, Commander Dowling had held his sub on the co-ordinates the hijacker had provided. The mood on the boat was tense to say the least, especially when the other senior officers knew Patel had taken control of the missiles. Several of them had quietly met with Pike and were keen to stop the hijackers. The Master at Arms felt he, and his small detachment of Marines could easily overpower Baine before he could deploy the deadly Ricin. But the orders from the Commander were clear.

'We wait for the Government's response,' said Pike.

'Yes, sir,' said one, 'but if they don't pay-up, and these bastards go for launch?'

First Officer Pike looked solemn. 'You know they have our families?'

'Yes, sir. But we cannot let them launch our birds.'

Pike looked at the faces of the men under his command. 'If the ransom is paid these guys should leave.'

'And if it's not and they go for a launch?'

'We kill them both and take our chances with the Ricin.'

No sooner had Pike finished speaking, than the boat's intercom sounded. 'First Officer Pike to the Officer's Mess. Mr Pike to the Officers Mess.'

Commander Dowling, Frank Baine, and Sir Anthony Grainger were already in the small mess room when Pike arrived. The politician looked gaunt and pale. Pike thought he could be on the edge of a heart attack. He guessed the pills the man kept taking were to control such an eventuality.

'Come in, Steve,' said Dowling, 'have a seat.'

'Well?' said Pike.

'We have received word from Downing Street. The ransom has been paid,' said Grainger.

'Yeah,' interrupted Baine, 'and more importantly I have just heard the transaction has gone through.'

'So you bastards will . . .'

Baine raised his hand to silence Pike. 'No need for insults, Mr Pike. We've all got what we wanted. Your very wise government has paid up, which means we'll soon be on our way.'

'And our families?' said Grainger.

'Will be released un-harmed, Sir Anthony, as soon as Mr Patel and myself are clear of Poseidon.'

'What now?' said Dowling?'

Baine stood up and looked at the three men. 'There is a helicopter on its way to this location as we speak. It should be here in,' he looked at his watch, 'just over the hour. In the meantime, let's all just relax and stay calm,' he pointed to his midriff and the Ricin concealed under his shirt. 'No need for anything nasty to happen now our business is concluded.'

'The sooner you're off my boat the better,' said Dowling.

'Oh, I agree,' smiled Baine.'

One hour and eight minutes later, the helicopter descended towards Poseidon. The three metre swell had the huge submarine heaving. It would not be easy to land the chopper on the foredeck and Baine was worried. He and Patel stood in front of the conning tower and braced themselves as the deck rose and fell below their feet. Commander Dowling, FO Pike, and Sir Anthony, watched from the top of the tower, as the pilot deftly brought the clattering aircraft closer and closer to the heaving deck. The engines screamed as the pilot expertly manipulated the throttle. Then, as if attracted by magnetic force, the helicopter touched down with a heavy metallic clunk. The pilot reduced the rotor speed and the chopper steadied, he turned and waved to the waiting hijackers. Baine and Patel moved along the deck in a slow comical crablike manner, compensating for the rise and fall of the foredeck. The pilot pushed open the door and yelled, 'Come on. This could slide off into the sea. Move it . . .'

Baine rushed forward as the deck fell away beneath his feet. Patel tripped over, dropping his bag. He crawled along the deck to retrieve it, but the pilot shouted again. 'Leave it f'godsake. Get your arse in here.

The little Indian abandoned the bag and crawled the last few feet to the helicopter, much to the delight of Dowling and Pike. 'Send a man out to retrieve that bag,' said Dowling.

The engines screamed as the pilot turned the throttle to full power, and the helicopter lifted effortlessly into the afternoon sky. The three men at the top of the tower watched in silence as the aircraft circled Poseidon.

'That's for you, Mr Baine, said the pilot, 'the boss said you'd have the combination.'

Baine smiled as he picked up the briefcase. He placed it on his lap, then looked out the window at the huge submarine a hundred feet below.

'What's this?' said Patel.

Baine smiled. 'Our bank account details, Ravinda. You'll be able to buy Kerala with your share.'

Baine spun the first tumbler and the lock sprung open. The click of the second tumbler was the last noise he ever heard.

The sudden explosion shocked the men on the tower. Instinctively they ducked below the steel parapet, as the helicopter disintegrated in a crimson ball of fire.

Chapter Twelve
'The Falcon'

The exertion of dragging the four bodies into the back room had Washington wheezing heavily. His face and body were new, but his heart was not, and he had to sit down until the dizziness abated and his breath steadied.

Back in the big room, he went to his bag and removed the Glock. He dropped the weapon's magazine and checked the ammunition. There was a cold breeze coming in through the front door now. The sun had disappeared, and the Welsh weather had reverted to type, with a fine drizzle chilling the air. He looked at the gun then moved to the staircase. On the first floor landing he cocked the weapon, slipping a round into the chamber with a metallic click. He took the balaclava from his pocket and pulled it over his already sweating head.

Mr and Mrs Pike stood in the centre of the room. The old man held his wife close. 'Do it quickly please,' he said.

Washington raised the gun and said, 'I don't want to hurt you. And if you behave you'll be on your way home very soon.'

Tears of relief ran down the old lady's face as her husband held her tightly.

'Let's go,' said the American. He waved the gun towards the landing, then handed the keys to the old man. 'Unlock the other doors please, George.'

The man did as instructed but continued to hold on to his trembling wife's hand. Lady Grainger and her daughter came out. The daughter screamed when she saw the masked gunman.

'Shut up,' shouted Washington, 'No one's gonna get hurt if you do as you're told.'

The old man unlocked the next door and Kathy Dowling and her two young sons emerged.

George Pike smiled weakly. 'It's all right. I think we could be going home.'

'Okay. Everybody downstairs, please,' said the American, 'but no funny business. This could still go wrong for you all.'

Lady Olivia Grainger put her arm around the shoulder of her sobbing daughter and walked down the stairs. Kathy Dowling and her boys were next, slowly followed by the Pikes.

In the big room Washington said, 'Okay. Everyone outside.'

The group huddled together as the drizzle soaked into their clothes.

'Into the barn,' said the American, as he waved the gun towards the ramshackle building a few yards away.

Kathy Dowling pulled open the old doors, the hinges creaking eerily.

'Everyone inside,' said Washington. He turned to the old man and said, 'The van. Keys are in the ignition. Go!'

No one moved. 'Get the hell outta here before I change my mind,' shouted the American.

George Pike helped his wife into the cab and then climbed in after her. The others all quickly piled into the rear and pulled the door closed. Pike started up the engine and eased the vehicle forward. As he slowly passed the American, he wound down the window and said, 'Thank you.'

The masked man lowered the gun and nodded, then pointed to the road at the edge of the farmyard. 'That way. It's about eleven miles to the village.'

Washington waited until the van was on its way down the hill, then slipped the gun into his waistband. He pulled off the uncomfortable balaclava and ran his hands though his hair and over his face. The rain had stopped, and a hint of sun was beginning to show through the breaking cloud. A swift movement in the sky caught his peripheral vision, and then there it was. The peregrine was back. He watched it swoop for a few seconds, and then he turned and went back into the barn. He picked up two heavy cans of petrol and humped them back into the house. He left one in the big room and took the other into the rear communications room. He stood for a moment looking at his former henchmen, then opened the can and poured the fuel over the bodies, being careful not to get any on himself. He spread the rest of the can around the backroom and threw the empty container in the corner.

The second can was carefully spread around the big room, with a trail leading towards the open door. The rank pungent smell made him gag, but the fresh air soon settled the feeling of nausea. He moved a few yards away from the door then took out a Zippo lighter. He could see the van weaving down the hill, over a mile away. The old man was driving carefully, as the road twisted and turned down the incline.

He flicked the lighter and the small yellow flame fluttered in the breeze. He threw the Zippo through the open door and quickly stepped back as the fuel caught and the flames appeared with a whoosh.

He watched for a few more seconds as the fire took hold, then quickly returned to the barn. In the corner was a large tarpaulin, which he carefully removed to reveal a powerful Yamaha motorcycle. He pushed the bike out, took the helmet from the handlebars and pulled it over his head. The bike fired up at the first press of the starter and the engine growled as he turned the throttle. The house was well ablaze now and the flames had totally engulfed the ground floor. The wooden floors and ceilings would go up like matchwood. There'd be nothing left except a blackened, solid stone carcass.

As he turned the bike towards the fields, the falcon flew overhead, then swooped a few yards away from him. Washington could clearly see its bright eyes as the elegant creature snared its prey. He waited until the bird flew off, then gunned the engine and headed across the fields.

At the bottom of the hill, George Pike brought the van to a stop and looked back at the thick pall of black smoke, rising into the evening sky like the plume from a rumbling volcano.

Chapter Thirteen
'Damage Control'

The subsequent forty-eight hours had been spent on damage control and containment.

HMS Poseidon had abandoned the short sea trial and returned to its base in Faslane. The crew to a man, had been de-briefed by Naval Security and, again to a man, had been reminded, they, as members of Her Majesty's Armed Forces, were subject to the stringent parameters of the Official Secrets Act.

Any breach of security and mention of recent events on Poseidon, by any member of its crew, would render said individual liable to a charge of treason, resulting in a minimum term of fourteen years imprisonment.

MI5, MI6, Special Branch and the National Counter Terrorism Office, had taken it in turn to interview the hostages. No real information, or intelligence had been forthcoming, other than; they all wore black coveralls and balaclavas. The leader spoke American and the others had East European accents.

After a rigorous twelve hours of questioning, Lady Grainger and her daughter Caroline, Kathy Dowling and her sons, along with the Pikes, were released, but not before they too had signed and been made aware of the consequences of breaching the Official Secrets Act.

Special Branch had taken over the investigation at the Welsh farmhouse, but the fire had, as was intended, destroyed anything that could offer a clue as to who the terrorists were. The four bodies were recovered but were burnt beyond recognition. DNA was extracted and sent for analysis, in the hope there may be a hit on the system to identify someone.

The van the hostages were given, had been dismantled and every inch of the vehicle had been inspected by the best forensic team in the country, resulting in absolutely nothing.

Nothing had appeared in the media . . . Yet.

Within an hour of the three billion pounds being paid, the Prime Minister had convened a meeting with the Director General of the Security Services. The meeting was brief.

The PM had stood in front of the big oak desk, her eyes narrowed, voice clear. 'I want you to bring all our assets to bear and find the perpetrators of this attack on our country. I want them all brought to justice, in whatever shape or form that justice maybe. Do you understand?'

The Director General nodded and said, 'Yes, ma'am, I . . .'

The PM raised her hand and continued. 'And I want our money back.'

Chapter Fourteen
'Nice Digs'

In his late-fifties, Jack Castle was tall, reasonably fit and healthy. That said, and according to his wife Nicole, losing a few pounds would not go amiss. He had a wicked sense of humour and an infectious personality which appealed to most people, although recently he was becoming less tolerant and somewhat short tempered.

The death of his parents on his 21st birthday had affected him very badly and, instead of pursuing his planned career in medicine, he'd joined the British Army. Fifteen years of hard work and dedication saw him rise to the rank of captain in the Special Air Service, after which, he'd moved into the world of private security. The company he'd joined all those years ago now belonged to him and, with the help of his partner and friend, Tom Hillman, they'd grown the business into a respected international entity.

The last three years however, had been interspersed with a couple of covert missions for British Intelligence.

Mathew Sterling was Jack's younger brother. They'd grown up in the north of England, in a beautiful home on the edge of Lake Windermere. Like Jack, Mathew also joined the army but trod a different path. He'd initially worked in Military Intelligence and then spent many years as a field operative. He too rose quickly through the security service and now, based in London's Vauxhall Cross building, he was head of MI6. For security reasons he'd chosen to use his mother's maiden name and for the last twenty years or so, had been known as Mr. Mathew Sterling.

In his 9th floor office, Mathew stood and looked out the window. The pleasure craft on the Thames, the busy traffic on Vauxhall Bridge and the hundreds of people going about their business. The knock on the door broke into his thoughts. 'Come in.'

'Mr Castle, sir.' said his secretary.

'Thank you, Victoria. Could you bring us some tea please?'

'Yes, sir.'

'Jack, great to see you,' said Mathew.

The two men smiled and embraced.

'You too, bro. How y'doin?' said Jack. Then looking around the office continued, 'and very nice digs by the way.'

Mathew nodded. 'Yes, it's not bad at all. You haven't been in here before have you?'

'No. Not since you were promoted. How's that going by the way?'

'Same shit, grander title.'

Jack smiled. 'Well, just one more step and you'll be Director General, mate. Then the knighthood eh?'

Mathew frowned. 'Not too sure about the knighthood, Jack. We are, after all, still commoners. We never went to the right schools.'

'Yeah, maybe. But I'm still counting on my little brother to uphold the family honour and pick up a 'Sir' at some point.'

They both laughed.

'Have a seat,' said Mathew, 'how's Nicole and my beautiful nieces?'

'A handful as usual,' smiled Jack, 'the twins are almost three now.'

'I know. I haven't seen them for ages. Soon as I get some time I'll come out for the weekend.'

'They always love to see Uncle Matt. And Nicole sends her love.'

Mathew smiled, then took a seat across from his brother.

It had taken over two hours to get from Jack's Berkshire home, in East Monkton, to Mathew's office and he was eager to know why his brother had asked him to come. 'So, what's the problem this time, Matt?'

'What, no more small talk, Jack?'

Jack leaned forward. 'You look tired, bro, and I'm sure you want to get right to business. You never ask me here unless you want me to help with something. So, what's up?'

The knock on the door was answered with a, 'Come in,' from Mathew. 'Thanks Victoria.'

The tea tray was placed in the table between the couches. 'Anything else, sir?'

Mathew smiled. 'Unless it's the DG, hold my calls for the next hour, please.'

'Yes, sir.'

Mathew sat back in the big leather Chesterfield. 'Okay. As usual, anything we say here is always top secret, but this one is exceptionally sensitive, Jack.'

Jack took a sip of the steaming tea, then said, 'I'm all ears, Matt.'

Chapter Fifteen
'Last Day'

'SIR ANTHONY RESIGNS' said the Daily Mail. 'GRAINGER ILL' said The Telegraph. 'PM LOSES CLOSEST ALLY' said The Times.

Lady Olivia Grainger looked across the breakfast table at her husband. 'You must eat something, darling.'

Sir Anthony looked gaunt and pale. His usual upbeat demeaner gone. There was a deep frown across his forehead as he read The Times editorial. 'Just tea this morning, Livvie.'

'The PM said there was no need for you to resign, darling. No one blames you for what happened.'

He folded the newspaper and dropped it on the floor. 'No one?'

'Please, Anthony, eat something.'

He stood up from the table and went to the window. There were still over a dozen reporters and cameramen out in the street. The young police officer just managing to keep them away from the steps in front of the elegant building.

As he looked out she heard him sigh. 'I've been tired of late, Livvie, and thinking of leaving government for some time. This has just been the catalyst, darling. And hardly my finest hour.'

'For God sake, Anthony, any man would have done the same with their families at risk.'

'That's what the PM said.'

'Well then, why on earth . . .'

He turned and raised his hand slightly, stopping her in mid-sentence. 'It's alright, Olivia. Really, it's all right.'

'I'm worried about you, Anthony. You really will make yourself ill.'

He looked at his wife. 'Well then what's in the papers will be true.'

'Darling I . . .'

'Please, Olivia, just let it go. Everything is going to be fine.'

He took out the pocket watch from his waistcoat. 'My car will be here shortly.'

'Have him come around to the mews entrance. You don't need to face those people at the front.'

He leaned down and kissed her cheek. 'Don't worry, my darling, I'll be fine.'

He took the jacket from the back of the chair and slipped it on. Turning to the big Ormolu mirror he adjusted his tie and waistcoat. 'How do I look?' he said with a smile.

Lady Grainger stood and put her arms around him. She held on for several seconds, then looked up into his eyes. 'I love you, my darling.'

'I love you too, Livvie.'

In the hallway he picked up his briefcase and went to the door. He stood for several seconds and then took a deep breath. As the door opened the pack of reporters rushed the steps, pushing aside the young constable. Grainger put his shoulders back and waited until Gary, and his driver forced their way through the mob of yelling journalists. With little regard for the news people the two burly security officers manoeuvred their charge through the clamouring mob and into the waiting Jaguar.

As the big car pulled away from the house Grainger said, 'Thank you gentlemen and good morning.'

'Morning, sir,' said the driver over his shoulder.

Gary turned and smiled. 'Good morning, Sir Anthony. Last day then, sir?'

Grainger looked out the window and across Green Park. 'Afraid so, Gary, last day indeed.'

The security officer turned again, the smile gone. 'I wish you'd let me come to Faslane with you, sir.'

Chapter Sixteen
'Follow the Money'

Jack's meeting with Mathew had been a revelation. He could not believe what his brother was saying. The Secretary of Defence gives terrorists access to a British nuclear submarine. Weapons systems breached. Three billion pounds paid.

'Jesus Christ, Mathew! Is this for real? Don't answer that, of course it is. You'd never bloody joke about something like this. And nothing in the papers?'

'Full national security blackout on this one, Jack.'

'So, was Grainger sacked?'

'Not privy to that. Sacked or resigned, either way he was finished. His failing health is obviously a cover story for the bloody press.'

Jack leaned back in the big Chesterfield and shook his head. 'This is unbelievable.'

Mathew grinned. 'They do say truth is stranger than fiction.'

'Yeah, I guess so. Okay, Mr Head of MI6. Why am I here?'

Mathew stood and went to his desk. He returned with a leather folder marked EYES ONLY. Jack grinned at the wording, and said, 'Here we go again.'

'The PM is monitoring this operation personally. If this gets out it's not just her job. It will bring down the government. She wants retribution. She's told the Director General that all assets are to be brought to bear, to capture or kill the people behind this attack.'

Jack grinned again. 'She actually said that? Capture or kill?'

'Probably not in those exact words, but that is the desired outcome.'

'The desired outcome?' Jack nodded and smiled. 'Right.'

'She also wants to recover the ransom.'

'Really? She doesn't want much then? But to be honest, Matt, this sounds like a job for a good detective. Not someone like me.'

'Perhaps. But I know you have all kinds of contacts. Especially in the, shall we say, less salubrious parts of the world. And then there's your father-in-law. Dimitri's intelligence network is almost as good as ours.'

Jack smiled. 'Yeah, well that does tend to be the case when you're one of the richest Russian oligarchs in the world.'

'The security services are stretched, Jack. In every arm of the service there's been cuts. We aren't as well-resourced as we once were.'

'No need to sell it, Matt. If I can help I will.'

'Are you sure? Nicole isn't gonna like it. The last time you helped us almost killed you.'

Jack gave a little chuckle. 'That's putting it mildly. But fuck it, I'm in bro. What's the plan?'

'MI5 is focussed on the UK, but I believe the answer is international.'

'Of course, it is. Whoever set this up is no muppet and they won't be anywhere near the UK now.'

'The money's the key, Jack. Follow the money and we'll find the people behind this.'

'Okay. So I guess I'm off to the Balkans?'

Mathew smiled. 'You're booked on the midnight flight to Podgorica, Montenegro.'

Chapter Seventeen
'Nicole'

Mathew had invited Jack to lunch at Vauxhall Cross's restaurant. Jack had dined there in the past and despite it being a typical 'executive dining facility' it was indeed one of the best restaurants in London. Normally he would have enjoyed the opportunity of a great meal with his brother, but with a midnight flight looming, he needed to get home to Nicole.

The tube and train journey from the city to East Monkton had been swifter than the earlier one and, with no commuters, the East Monkton train was relatively quiet, giving Jack time to think about the mission he'd been asked to undertake. Mathew said the only real intelligence was the initial destination of the ransom payment and the information from the hostages, stating the 'leader' was American, or at least spoke with an American accent.

The burning of the Welsh farmhouse and the destruction of the helicopter to destroy all evidence, spoke to the ruthlessness of the person, or persons, behind the heist. He smiled to himself at the use of the American colloquialism. His thoughts continued. He was puzzled why the 'leader' had let the hostages go. Why free them to pass on information? He was obviously ruthless enough to murder his colleagues, but compassionate enough to let the civilians go. That was it . . . they were civilians. Whoever the leader was, he had a code, not your average hi-jacking terrorist. So maybe he was ex-military, maybe ex-security services? Who knows? And was he really an American?

Mathew had agents in America working that angle, but Jack had his own contacts in the States, and would call on them if need be. His focus, for the moment, was the Balkans and he'd definitely need some 'specialist' help there. He took out his smartphone, swiped the screen and found the number. It took several rings until a deep voice said, 'Da?'

The service pulled into the little station at East Monkton, just after 2 o'clock. Only Jack and a couple of ladies, who'd obviously been shopping in the city, exited the train. The station was now un-manned, and the tiny booking office closed-up, replaced by a ticket machine. Jack found himself missing the cheery smile of the old guy who used to welcome everyone through the gate.

The lights on the Jaguar flashed as he pressed the key-fob. He climbed in and, for a few seconds, relished the new car smell. The big engine gurgled into life and he backed out of the carpark. A little under ten minutes later, he pulled up in front of the big house.

Nicole Elizabeth Orlova, was born of an English mother and Russian father. She and Jack had been together for over twenty years, the last four of which as husband and wife.

At thirty-nine years old, she had inherited her dead mother's beauty and her father's shrewd brain. In her younger years she'd been a very successful fashion model in Moscow, but now was a respected business woman with a chain of spas, and a very lucrative property portfolio in England and Europe. Her father was the billionaire Russian oligarch, Dimitri Mikhailovich Orlov.

She was in the garden snipping away at some roses bushes, her smartphone wedged between her cheek and shoulder, talking ten-to-the-dozen in Russian as Jack approached. She finished the call and slipped the phone into her shorts pocket, pulled off her gloves and dropped them and the secateurs onto the lawn.

Jack smiled at her outfit. Bare feet, cut-off denim shorts, a baggy white T-shirt and, with her blonde hair tied back in a ponytail, looking ten years younger than her age.

As he kissed her he got the faint smell of Christian Dior. 'Hi baby.'

She smiled and linked her arm through his as they walked back to the house. 'You left early, Jack?'

'Yeah, I had to see Mathew. He sends his love to you and the twins.'

She turned to him, a slight frown on her beautiful face. 'Oh, well that's lovely, but what did he really want?'

Jack looked sheepish. 'Err, it's just a little job in the Balkans. Nothing dangerous.'

She stopped and punched him on the arm. 'The Balkans? You said you wouldn't do any more work for Mathew. Especially after the last time, Jack.'

'I know baby, but like I said, it's nothing dangerous, just a few enquiries.'

She folded her arms and looked stern. 'Enquiries? Right. Like I'm gonna believe that?'

Chapter Eighteen
'No Visa Required'

The rest of the day was spent with Nicole and the twins. After supper Svetlana, the nanny, took the girls off to bed, leaving Jack and Nicole out on the big patio overlooking the lake. It was a warm evening and, even at this distance, the dragon-flies could be seen skimming across the still silvery water.

'What time are you leaving, darling?'

'Mathew's sending a car. Should be here about nine o'clock.'

She looked at her watch, it was a few minutes past seven. 'You'd better go on up and get ready then?'

'There's plenty of time yet, babe.'

She stood up, came over and sat on his lap, then wrapped her arms around his neck. Her voice had a husky timbre. 'I really do think you should go up, Jack.'

He looked into her beautiful eyes and smiled. 'I think you're right.'

The car pulled up to the front of the big house a few minutes before nine. Nicole had wanted to come out to Heathrow with him, but Jack had said, 'It's fine baby. No need for you to schlep all the way out there.'

The young driver took Jack's small wheelie and put it in the boot, then opened the rear door.

'I'll sit up front, son.'

'Okay, sir.'

Jack turned to Nicole and held her face in his hands. 'I'll call you before I fly, and once I land.'

'Be careful, darling. I love you.'

'I love you too, baby. See you soon.'

She watched as the car drove to the gates and then returned his wave.

'Take care, my love,' she said quietly.

The Polish Airlines flight to Montenegro was delayed. The aircraft had developed a 'technical problem' but this was expected to be resolved within the next hour. He'd flown many of the world's airlines and was used to such issues. Where once it never worried him now, with a family, he was more concerned about putting his life in the hands of faceless entities.

The Business Class Lounge was busy, and it was clear the flight would be full, that said he was tired and hoped to get some sleep once onboard. It was almost midnight when the announcement to board eventually came.

The flight took a little under three hours, and after what turned out to be a decent meal, served by the two very attentive and attractive stewardess, Jack did manage to sleep for an hour or so.

Golubovci Airport is one of two international airports in Montenegro and is situated about seven miles south of the city of Podgorica. The new Terminal 2 which opened in 2006 was to say the least impressive. Jack's transition through immigration and customs was not swift, but, as no visa is required for British subjects, hassle free. He quickly made his way to the exit and was pleased to see dozens of taxis readily available for the short ride into the city.

As part of his cover, Jack had asked Mathew's secretary to book him a suite at the elegant Nova Varos Hotel, on the West bank of the Ribnica River. This area, referred to as the 'New Town' district, was inhabited and frequented by the more prosperous and influential citizens of Podgorica. This area was also the hub of Montenegro's banking and financial system.

The drive from the airport was swift and, although the early morning traffic was building, the driver still managed to get Jack to the hotel in a little over ten minutes.

The taxi came to a stop under the elegant portico. A young valet rushed to open the door as Jack climbed out. 'Good morning, sir, Welcome to the Nova Varos.'

Jack nodded. 'Good morning,' then added, 'It's fine,' when the valet attempted to carry his luggage.

After checking-in, the same valet escorted Jack to his room and, in excellent English, gave the customary spiel about the suite's facilities.

Jack nodded, said, 'Thanks, son,' then handed over a ten euro note.

After the kid had gone, Jack checked his Rolex, and although it was still only 4am in the UK, made the call to Nicole.

'Jack?' her voice was thick with sleep.

'Hi, baby. I'm at the hotel. It's early so go back to sleep.'

'You okay, darling?'

'I'm fine, baby. Going to see if I can get a couple of hours sleep myself.'

'Okay. Good night.'

'Good morning, baby.'

He heard her chuckle and the line went silent.

Chapter Nineteen
'Dead As Disco'

For the last five years Sir Anthony Grainger had woken at 5am. In the winter months he spent the first forty-five minutes of his day on the running machine in the basement. In the spring and summer however, come rain or shine, he ran in nearby Green Park. He'd just finished the final circuit and was at the side of the road, jogging on the spot, waiting for a couple of cars to pass. The screeching sound of the moped's engine, as the rider accelerated towards him, startled Grainger. Then, above the clatter of the moped, three shots rang-out.

The first bullet missed and hit the nearby Royal Mail post-box, carving a large chunk out of the freshly painted icon. The second bullet shattered his clavicle, causing him to spin around, a scream of pain coming from deep in his throat. The third bullet smashed into his back, lodging in the scapula and knocking him to the floor.

The man on the back of the moped watched as the Knight of the Realm crashed to the pavement, motionless, then screamed at the driver, 'He's fuckin gone!'

Two hours later Rick Washington waited impatiently. The old warehouse East of the River Thames had been closed-up for years and was due for demolition. The area soon to be developed for upmarket apartment blocks. He looked at his watch again. They were late. 'Where are these fuckers?' he said out loud. Then he heard the clatter of the moped's engine.

The two youths drove into the ramshackle building and screeched to a halt in a cloud of dust and petrol fumes. Washington stepped to one side as the smoke from the exhaust drifted past him. 'You're fucking late.'

'Chill out, man,' said the driver.

'Yeah, chill, man,' said the shooter.

'Is he dead?' said Washington.

The shooter laughed. 'Dead as disco, mate,' then the two kids high-fived each other.

'Okay, good. And the weapon?'

'In the Thames, man. Just like you said.'

'Okay, guys,' said Washington, 'you did good,' He threw an envelope to the driver. 'Here's your money.'

The driver quickly checked the envelope and grinned. He showed the bundle of notes to his companion and they both high-fived again.

'And here's a little bonus,' said the American, as he threw over a small plastic bag.

The shooter caught it and held it up, shaking the pills within. 'What's this mate?'

Washington grinned this time. 'Only the best E's in London. Knock yourself out. It's party time.'

The two youths again hit the high-five, climbed on the moped and clattered away in a cloud of dust and fumes.

The media was awash with the news of the horrific shooting of Sir Anthony Grainger. Rick Washington read the paper and was a very unhappy man. Yes, Sir

76

Anthony had been shot twice, but he was not dead. He'd been taken to hospital and was now in a serious, but stable condition. The operating surgeon had made a TV announcement on the steps of the hospital. His statement made it clear his patient was strong and in the best place to ensure a full recovery.

In a rage, Washington threw the paper to the floor, as the pages spread out across the carpet he bent down and picked up one of them. He read a short piece about two young men who'd been found dead in the East End of London. First indications were they'd died from a toxic chemical. A small quantity of tablets had been found and were being analysed. A police officer had commented that the pills were most likely the cause of death.

'Not all bad news then,' said Washington.

Chapter Twenty
'Mike Vogler'

The hospital reception area was extremely busy and with only two people at the desk, dealing with visitors, telephones, and questions from medical staff, somewhat chaotic.

Rick Washington waited patiently in the queue confident in his disguise. A light brown wig covered his own black hair, thick rimmed glasses and a false moustache changed his facial appearance. The padded oversize jacket made him look fatter than he was. His tradecraft as an ex-CIA agent told him people will only remember the obvious.

The queue moved slowly forward. The American smiled when the old man in front grumbled, 'Bloody NHS. Not what it used to be.'

A few minutes later he was at the desk. He leaned over and with a charming smile said quietly, 'Good morning. I'm from the American Embassy. I'm here to see Sir Anthony Grainger. Could you tell me where I could find him, please?'

The flustered woman looked impressed for a moment, then scanned the monitor in front of her. She too leaned forward and said quietly, 'Intensive Care, First floor, sir.'

Washington flashed the smile again, 'Thank you, ma'am.'

He rode the lift to the first floor and went to the Ward Sister's desk. The same charm was used. 'Good morning. I'm Mike Vogler. I'm from the American Embassy. The Ambassador has asked me to visit Sir Anthony Grainger. The Ambassador is an old friend and keen to know how Sir Anthony is doing.'

This woman was not the harassed person from down stairs, and said, 'Do you have some identification, please?'

'Yes, ma'am.' Washington flashed an American Embassy wallet and showed the fake Mike Vogler ID.

'He's in room five. He's still very groggy from the operation. But you may see him for five minutes,' her tone was stern. 'Five minutes and no more now.'

'No problem. Thank you, ma'am.'

At the door to room five, Washington waited while the attending nurse finished her checks. As she passed him he smiled, and said, 'Good morning.'

She returned the smile and he watched as she disappeared around the corner. He entered the room and quietly closed the door. Grainger looked to be sleeping. Several tubes going in and out of his body were hooked up to various monitors. At the bedside Washington checked the screens. The man's vital signs showed a constant, but low heart-rate. He took a seat next to the bed and gently laid his hand on Grainger's upper arm. 'Sir Anthony? Sir Anthony?'

Grainger sucked in a deep breath and slowly opened his eyes. For a second he didn't know the man at his bedside . . . and then, even through the disguise, he recognised Washington.

'What . . .'

The American put his finger to Grainger's lips. 'Shhh, Sir Anthony. Don't speak. I'm just here to let you know you'll never see your share of the ransom.'

'But . . .'

'Shhh.' The finger was on the lips again. 'but I must thank you for all your help. Your idea of kidnapping your own family was genius, sir. But it's time for me go.'

'But I . . .'

This time Washington's full hand replaced the finger and covered Grainger's nose and mouth. The older man struggled, but in his weakened condition his exertions only hastened the outcome. It took less than a minute for Sir Anthony Grainger to die.

Chapter Twenty One
'Mikhail Gorbachev'

It was a little before 11am, when his smartphone startled Jack awake. 'Mathew?'

'Jack, hi. Were you sleeping?'

'Yeah, but it's okay. Whatsup?'

'There's been a development. Sir Anthony Grainger was shot.'

'Jesus, is he okay?'

'No. He's dead, Jack. But not from his wounds.'

'What?'

'He was shot while out jogging. A couple of kids on a moped. But he survived. He was in intensive care. Then someone walked in this morning and killed him.'

'So, the moped shooters were not random. It was a hit.'

Certainly looks like it and, since they botched it, whoever wanted Grainger dead came back, or sent someone, to finish the job.'

'Right. But again, why?'

'We don't know yet but, it may well be related to Poseidon.'

'The hospital will have CCTV. Is there any sight of this morning's killer?'

'Special Branch are going through the tapes. Soon as they have something they'll send it over to us.'

'Okay. Send anything you get to my phone. Anything else, Matt?'

'Yes. The bruising on his cheeks and mouth indicate suffocation.'

'Nasty way for the old boy to go.'

'But it may give us a break. We may be able to pull some DNA.'

'Okay, good. Let me know if anything comes up from that.'

The house phone rang.

'Matt I gotta go. Talk soon.'

'Okay, Take care, Jack.'

He reached over and picked up the house phone. 'Hello?'

'Good morning, sir, this is reception. There is a Mr Mikhail Gorbachev to see you.'

Jack smiled. 'Please ask him to come up.'

'Certainly, sir, Thank you.'

A few minutes later, a hefty knock on the door made Jack smile again. He opened the door and said to the big man in front of him, 'Mikhail Gorbachev? Really?'

The big man grinned, then bear-hugged Jack. 'Is good to see you again, boss.'

After being released from the crushing hug, Jack said, 'Bogdan Markov. My old friend. It's great to see you too, buddy.'

Bogdan Markov was almost sixty, a big man with a cheerful face that belied his tough character. In his younger days he'd been a helicopter pilot with the Spetznaz, the Russian Special Forces. Jack Castle first met him in Kosovo after he'd left the Soviet military.

Bogdan was working as a mercenary and had managed to secure himself a lucrative contract as a mountain guide working for the United Nations. Markov had joined Jack's team for a covert mission on the Kosovo border, that resulted in the neutralisation of a particularly nasty Armenian warlord. It was on that mission a mutual respect and lasting friendship had developed. Jack had last seen Bogdan over two year ago, when they'd worked together on the *Beirut Shahadi* operation. Now and for the last few years, his old friend had been working on the fringes of the Moscow Mafia. Bogdan also owned and operated a very trendy and exclusive night club in Moscow's Metropolitan Hotel.

'So, boss. What's the deal?'

Jack smiled. 'What? No small talk? No chit-chat?'

The Russian laughed out loud. 'Da. You English, always love the chit-chat.'

Jack smiled again. 'How's your brother, Grigory?'

'Da. He is very well. His restaurant does good business now with many rich Russians.'

'And you, my friend. You are well? Business is good? The club is good?'

'Da, da. All is good, boss. I have two clubs now, thanks to you.'

'Me?' How's that?'

'The last job we work together. That bastard Vinni Shahadi. The five million dollars you give me. I buy second club.'

Jack nodded. 'Well, it wasn't strictly me who gave it, my friend. It was Shahadi's money.'

'Da. But this bastard is now dead. So fuck him.'

They both laughed.

'Okay boss. So, we talk now about the job now?'

Jack smiled. 'Da, Bogdan. We talk about the job now.'

Jack didn't mention the hi-jacking of Poseidon to Bogdan. Not because he didn't trust him, simply because he knew his old friend. The Russian liked a drink and there may well come a time, with a litre of vodka under his belt, that the big man could inadvertently blurt it out to someone. As far as Bogdan was concerned a person, or persons, yet unknown had kidnapped British citizens and a ransom had been paid. The job was to find the perpetrators and, if possible, the money.

'B'lyaad,' said Bogdan. 'Who did they kidnap for such money? It was the Queen, da?'

Jack laughed at the Russian profanity and the thought HRH ever being kidnapped. 'No, my friend, not her majesty. Who it was doesn't matter now. The people behind all this are who we're after.'

Bogdan winked. 'And the money too, boss.'

'If we find the money it'll have to be returned to the British Government, buddy. But don't worry, I'm sure there'll be a very handsome reward.'

The Russian grinned. 'Okay, if there is money for Bogdan, I will be happy. If no money for Bogdan, is niet problem. I am happy to be with you, my friend. We will have some fun for sure. Da?'

Jack stood up, slapped the big man on the back, and said, 'Right. Let's go see this bloody banker.'

Chapter Twenty Two
'The Henagar'

It was a little before midday when Jack and Bogdan left the Nova Varos Hotel. The temperature had crept up and was now over 30 centigrade, with the warmest part of the day yet to come. It was only about ten minutes' walk from the hotel to the bank, so they never took up the valet's offer to secure them a taxi. A decision they regretted after walking for a couple of minutes. Jack in slacks and a shirt was hot, but Bogdan, still wearing his Armani leather jacket, looked ready to boil.

The big man's appearance did however fit-in with Jack's cover as a wealthy business man wishing to use the bank's extremely discreet service. Bogdan looked every bit the very capable and threatening minder.

The Henagar Merchant Bank is not one of the largest financial establishments in Montenegro. It is however one of the richest. The Henagar family were old world Balkan aristocracy who'd established the bank back in the mid 1800's. Unfortunately, and due to the mismanagement of Borat Henagar's eldest grandson, the business began to fail in the 1970's.

At the height of the cold war, the bank was taken over by a small group of forward thinking Russian businessmen, allegedly high-ranking KGB and Politburo members, who turned the business around. By the time the Russian Federation shattered in 1992 the bank had re-established its premier position as one of the world's most secure and discreet merchant banks, largely due to the fact it was happy, and willing, to deal with the most unsavoury of individuals, from African dictators to international terrorists.

All this of course, behind closed doors, and within the realms of respectability originally established by old Borat Henagar, who would surely be spinning in his grave, if he knew what the institution he'd created had become.

It was Bogdan who, with information from his Mafia boss in Moscow, had discovered the Henagar was more than likely the bank through which the ransom had been administered.

It took a little over fifteen minutes to find the bank. The original building, in the old part of the city, had been turned into a trendy bistro and wine bar. The Henagar now ran its business from a very modern establishment in the New Town area, right in the heart of the financial district.

Large tinted glass doors were monitored by three sets of CCTV cameras. As the two approached, a small screen, to the side of the doors, lit up and gave access to an intercom.

Jack touched the screen and said, 'I'm here to establish an account.'

No reply came, but within a second or two of Jack's words, the doors slid silently open.

They stepped into a large hallway and the outer doors slid closed behind them. The internal doors were not tinted, and Jack could see a burly security guard on the other side. The internal doors opened.

'Good afternoon, gentlemen,' said the guard. Then pointing to an elegant desk a few yards away, said, 'Please.'

A very attractive middle-aged woman stood as they approached the desk. She looked directly at Jack, and said, 'Good afternoon, sir. How may we help you?'

Jack smiled. 'I'd like to talk to the Managing Director please.'

'Yes, sir. And I believe you wish to establish an account?'

'That's correct.'

'Our General Manager would be able to help you with that, sir.'

Jack's smile faded. 'I'd prefer to deal with the most senior person in the bank.'

'Of course, sir. May I have your name please.'

Jack's smile returned. 'Smith.'

Bogdan grinned.

The big office on the sixth floor was modern yet elegant, with a view that looked out over the winding river.

'Good afternoon, gentlemen. I am Emilio Schlovan,' said the MD.

Jack smiled and held out his hand. 'Jack Smith.' He didn't introduce Bogdan.

The banker nodded slightly and returned the smile. 'Mr Smith. Yes of course. Please have a seat. May I offer you a drink?'

'Just water, please,' said Jack.

Schlovan spoke into the intercom. 'Water please, Katarina.'

A few seconds later a young woman entered with a tray. She placed a bottle of water and a crystal tumbler in front of Jack and Bogdan. Smiled then left the room.

After the door closed, Shlovan said. 'Now . . . Mr Smith. How may we help you, sir?'

Jack filled the tumbler with water and drank half of it down. 'I have interests in South America, America and Europe. And as our business has grown so rapidly we have an issue with money.'

The banker smiled. 'Not the lack of it I suspect?'

Jack finished the water. 'On the contrary, Mr Schlovan.'

'Please, call me Silvio. And what type of assistance do you require from us, sir?'

'We have to move funds from North America and Europe, which would then need to be worked or invested in multiple legitimate enterprises.'

Schlovan nodded sagely. 'May I ask what kind of volume we are talking, Mr Smith?'

Jack turned to Bogdan. 'Mikael?'

The Russian paused for a few seconds. 'About fifteen million dollars.'

Schlovan looked mildly disappointed. 'No disrespect intended, sir. But that's a very simple amount for us to handle for you.'

'A week,' said Bogdan.'

The banker's eyes widened. 'Ahh. Yes of course, sir. It'll take a day or two for us to put a prospectus together. We want to make sure your funds are disbursed and invested in the best possible way. How long will you be in Montenegro?'

'A few days,' said Jack.

'Very well. I'm having a small gathering at my home this evening. I would be honoured if you could join us?'

Jack stood up. 'That's very kind. We'd be happy to.'

'If you let Katarina know your hotel, she will arrange a car to pick you up. Shall we say nine o'clock?'

Jack and the banker shook hands. 'Thank you, Silvio. Until this evening then.'

Chapter Twenty Three
'An Old Acquaintance'

It was late afternoon when Jack called Nicole. Bogdan had gone back to his room for a nap and Jack had just showered. The heat of the day had past and the temperature was now a pleasant 20 centigrade. The balcony windows were open and the light breeze from the river freshened the room.

'How are the girls, darling?'

'Missing their daddy, as always.'

Jack smiled. 'Me too, baby.'

'How's the hotel?'

'It's fine. Bogdan sends his regards, by the way.'

He heard her little laugh. 'How is the big man?'

'Same as always.'

'Tell him I said he has to look after you.'

Jack smiled. 'Yes, boss.'

'I love you, Zaikin.'

His fone beeped to signal another call. 'Love you too, baby. Sorry, gotta go. Call comin' in. Talk soon, darling.'

'Take care, Jack.'

'Always.'

Jack looked at the screen, swiped it, and said, 'Hi Matt.'

'Jack, hello. You okay?'

'I'm good. Whatsup?'

'We got forensics back from Special Branch. They got a hit on the DNA from Sir Anthony's body.'

'Excellent. Anyone we know?'

'Yes, indeed. Looks to be an old acquaintance of yours.'

'Really?'

'Yes. Our old friend, Greg Stoneham.'

'Jesus, Matt. Are they sure?'

'Ninety-nine-point-nine percent sure.' The line was silent for several seconds . . . 'Jack?'

'I'm here Matt. What about the CCTV? He's not that stupid to be caught on camera.'

'We have a copy of the tapes. But the man that entered the hospital looks nothing like Stoneham.'

'He'd be in disguise.'

'Of course, he would. He's a pro and knows his street-craft. But the man on the tape doesn't resemble Stoneham in any way at all. He doesn't even limp.'

'But it's definitely Stoneham's DNA on the body?'

'Yes.' The line was silent again . . . 'Jack?'

'Yeah, I'm here. If that bastard's involved, then you can definitely say Sir Anthony's murder and the Poseidon hijacking are related.'

'Certainly looks that way.'

'Okay, thanks, Mathew. Have you told the Americans?'

'Not yet. But we'll be making that call very soon. They still have him on their Most Wanted List. And since he killed those two police officers in Istanbul, so does Interpol.'

'Right, so at least we know who we're after. Send me the hospital footage, please.'

'Will do. Any developments your end, Jack?'

'We've contacted the banker and are invited to a party tonight.'

'Okay good. I'll let you go, Be careful eh?'

Jack smiled. 'Always.'

'Talk soon, Jack.'

'Cheers. bro.'

The line went silent.

Chapter Twenty Four
'Just Information'

It took a little over thirty minutes to drive from the city to the affluent area of Ponari on the north shore of Lake Scutari. The banker's home was opulent to say the least, with a high perimeter wall and heavy security gates. Their car pulled up to the front portico and the chauffer quickly jumped out to open the door for Jack. The evening was warm with a clear sky, and a full moon illuminating the luxurious gardens. In the shadows, cast by the mature trees, Jack could see, what he surmised to be, at least three security men.

As they entered the large hall, a young man greeted them and said, 'Good evening and welcome, gentlemen. Please come this way.'

They followed the flunky along a marble hallway, past a large curving staircase and into the main drawing room. The big double doors were open, and Jack could see there were probably 40 or 50 guests assembled. He turned to Bogdan and said quietly, 'Just a small gathering eh?'

As they entered the elegant room, Silvio Schlovan immediately left the group he was chatting with, and scurried over to welcome Jack. 'Mr Smith,' he said with a knowing smile. He offered his hand, and as they shook, continued. 'Welcome to my humble home.'

'Thank you, Silvio.'

The banker nodded to Bogdan. 'And good evening to you, Mikael.' No handshake was offered.

Bogdan smiled and looked the man straight in the eyes. *I hope I get to kick your ass, you fucka,* he thought to himself.

Schlovan turned and said, 'Let me introduce you to some interesting people, Mr Smith.'

'Please. Call me Jack.'

The banker's knowing smile returned. 'Jack . . . Yes, of course.'

The banker, a permanent smile on his round face, presented Jack to various men in the room. 'This is, Jack. Soon to be a very special client and hopefully a future friend.'

Jack nodded, smiled, shook hands, and made small talk, as the sycophant Silvio continued to parade him around the assembled guests, with Bogdan, ever at Jack's shoulder, looking somewhat menacing.

Finally, Jack was introduced to the banker's wife. 'Esther, may I introduce, Jack. Jack this is Esther, my wife.'

Jack smiled and gently shook the offered hand. 'My pleasure, Esther.'

'Welcome to our home.'

He felt her hold onto his hand for longer than necessary, as her beautiful eyes held his gaze. She was perhaps 35 or 36, and at least twenty years younger than the banker.

'You have a beautiful home, Esther.'

'Yes, thank you. We do love the place.'

94

The party progressed into the evening and although there was no formal dinner, a sumptuous buffet had been provided, which the big Russian made full use of.

Jack had made it clear he wished to stay on after the party to discuss business. A request the banker was more than happy to comply with. It was after 1 o'clock, when the last guests were waved off by Schlovan and he returned to the drawing room.

Bogdan was sitting at the other end of a large chaise, chatting to Esther. Jack stood at the big patio windows looking out into the gardens. He could see at least one security guard patrolling the grounds.

'Esther,' said the banker, 'I need to talk to Jack for a little while. Why don't you go on up, my darling?'

Before she could answer, Bogdan was alongside her, a switch-blade in his hand. The steel glinted under the light from the huge chandelier.

'Sit down, Silvio,' said Jack, as he pulled the heavy drapes across the patio windows.

'What the hell . . .?'

'Shut up and sit down,' said Jack menacingly.

The banker took a seat opposite his trembling wife. Jack moved quickly to the big double doors and closed them, the tie-back cord from the curtains in his hand.

'You are crazy if you . . .'

'I said shut the fuck up,' snapped Jack, then quickly came over and used the cord to secure the red-faced bankers wrists to the arms of the chair.

Tears ran down the woman's face, as the big Russian placed the tip of the knife on her cheek.

Jack put his most serious face on and looked Schlovan in the eyes. 'Mikael here was in this part of the world during the late unpleasantness. He was one of Dushan Grasic's interrogators. You remember Dushan Grasic don't you, Silvio?'

The banker, his red face now fearfully pale, shook his head.

'Ah, okay. Well, Grasic was one of the more sadistic war criminals during the Balkan War. He was one of the top-ten most wanted, once the war was over. Ring any bells, Silvio?'

Again, the terrified banker shook his head. 'No, I . . .'

'Not to worry. It's not important. What is important, and you must understand this, Silvio, Mikael here was Grasic's favourite. He could torture a person for days, and still manage to keep them alive.'

'Oh, God. Please don't . . .'

'Shhh. Just calm down and listen. All we need is a little information, then you and your lovely wife will be free, and we'll be gone.'

The man, tears rolling down his cheeks nodded . . . 'Yes, yes anything.'

'Good, good. Take a deep breath. Relax and focus.'

The man sucked in a lungful of air, then let out a huge sigh, as Bogdan removed the knife from his wife's tear-soaked cheek.

'You have a study here?'

'Yes, yes, I do.'

'And you can log-on to the bank's server?'

'Yes. But I can't transfer any funds. You won't be able to steal anything.'

'We don't want money, Silvio.'

'Then what do . . .'

Jack held up his hand. 'Just information.'

'But I . . .'

Jack raised his hand again and smiled. 'Let's all go to your study, shall we?'

Bogdan took hold of the woman's arm and helped her to her feet, as she looked like she was about to faint. He bent down and deftly slit through the cords that secured the bankers wrists.

'After you, Silvio,' said Jack, 'and please don't try anything foolish. We're not here to kill anyone. But that all depends on you. Whether you live or die tonight is entirely up to you.'

'Yes, yes, this way, this way.'

As the group left the drawing room, Jack caught Bogdan's wink.

The study was as elegant as the rest of the house, with a huge antique mahogany desk in the corner. Jack quickly closed the drapes and said, 'Log-on.'

Bogdan helped the woman to a chair and stood behind her, his hand resting on her bare shoulder, the knife inches away from the side of her face.

'I'm in,' said Schlovan.

Jack sat on the corner of the desk and turned the screen, so he could see as well. 'There was a transaction a couple of days ago. Three billion pounds came into your bank.'

The pale face had returned to its usual red, and the banker looked up. 'I . . .'

Jack put his hand on the man's shoulder. 'All I want to know is where the three billion went to, Silvio.'

'I can't bring it back, I . . .'

Jack squeezed the shoulder. 'I just want to know where it went.'

'And be fucking quick about it,' snapped Bogdan, waving the knife in the woman's face.

'Yes, yes, I'm sorry . . .'

Jack turned his head away and smiled at Bogdan's outburst.

The banker deftly tapped at the keyboard and a few minutes later said, 'Here.'

Jack read the screen. 'So, it's evenly disbursed between three accounts.'

'Yes.'

'Less three million pounds?'

'Yes. Our commission.'

'Wow, we're in the wrong fuckin business,' said Bogdan.

Jack smiled at his friend's comment. 'You can keep your commission, Silvio.'

'Is that all you . . .?'

The pressure increased on the shoulder. 'Where are those banks?'

'I can't . . .'

Again, the pressure. 'I know all about number accounts my friend, and you guys always know where the money moves to. So, where the fuck are those banks?'

Schlovan tapped away again, then pointed to the screen. 'There.'

'Good. Now that wasn't too difficult was it?'

The banker leaned back in his chair, a look of exhaustion on his big round face. Jack took out his smartphone and snapped a picture of the screen. 'And that concludes our business. Thank you, Silvio.'

'You won't get away with this, you know?'

Jack smiled. 'What, you mean legally? I don't think you'll be bringing-in any financial authorities. Do you?'

'Do you know who owns, The Henagar?' said the banker, somewhat emboldened.

Jack smiled. 'Actually, we do. And your bosses aren't going to be very happy if they find out you've co-operated with us so, willingly, shall we say?'

The banker swallowed deeply. 'You've got what you came for. Now what?'

'Now,' said Jack. 'We'll bid you good-night.'

The banker stood, went over to his wife, and wrapped his arm around her shoulders, then looked at Bogdan.

'Boo!' said the big Russian.

The couple flinched simultaneously at the taunt. Bogan smiled and said. 'Dasvidanya.'

'Oh,' said Jack. 'You wouldn't mind if we used your chauffer to take us back into town, would you, Silvio?'

The banker never answered.

Chapter Twenty Five
'Do Not Disturb'

It was well after 2am when they arrived back at the Nova Varos, but the hotel was still busy, largely due to the swish nightclub on the top floor.

'How about an hour in the club, boss?'

Jack patted the big man on the back. 'I'll pass, if that's okay, buddy? But you go. I'll see you at breakfast. Nine o'clock okay?'

'Da, okay boss. See you in morning.'

Jack took the house elevator, and Bogdan joined the short queue for the express-lift to the roof-top club.

As the doors closed Jack checked his Rolex, 02:35, too late to ring Nicole. The lift came to a stop with a slight jerk and the doors slid quietly open. At the end of the long corridor he touched the key-card to the panel and the door clicked open. He stepped into the room, and just caught sight of the shadow, before feeling the pain, and then slipping into oblivion . . .

The stinging slap across his face brought him round. He moaned as he opened his eyes and the pain hit him again. His head was pounding, a trickle of warm blood ran down the back of his neck.

Two men stood in front of him. Thirties, fit, and mean. The taller one spoke first. 'Wakey, wakey, man.'

'I didn't call for room service,' groaned Jack.

The smaller, stockier one, punched him hard in the ribs.

Jack sucked in a lung-full of air and groaned again. 'No tip for you, mate.'

The man made to strike, but the other snapped, 'Enough!'

'You, I'll tip,' said Jack.

'You're a funny guy,' said the man in charge.

Jack held one hand to the back of his head, the other against his ribs. 'What can I do for you?'

'You can start by telling us who the fuck you are, and who you're working for?'

Jack looked around the room. It had obviously been searched. 'Smith, Jack Smith.'

'You checked in as, Mr Mason,' then waving a passport said, 'and this was in the fridge. Also, in the name of, Mason. Who hides their passport in a fridge?'

'Okay, so I'm, Jack Mason.'

'This passport looks brand-new, yet it has many stamps and visas. You can get entry to many countries with this. So, who are you really, Jack? If that's your real name.'

'So it's a new passport, so what. Yeah, I travel a lot. And sure, you can call me, Jack. You can call me anything you like . . . as long as it's not *darling*.'

The taller nodded to the shorter, and this time the punch knocked all the wind out of Jack.

'Keep joking, Jack. My friend here can use you as a punch bag all night. Now who the fuck are you really? British Intelligence?'

It took a few seconds for Jack to get his breath back, he looked up at the man and said, 'My name is Smith . . . no, Mason . . . no . . . oh, fuck it, what the hell, just call me, darling.'

The fist was raised again. 'Stop.'

The little guy looked disappointed.

'Let's take him back. On your feet, Jack.'

Jack stood, as the little guy produced a silenced Smith & Wesson revolver.

They moved to the door and the leader opened it. Bogdan Markov stood in front of them, clenched fist raised, ready to knock on the door. For a split second no one moved. Then, as fast as a flyweight boxer, the big Russian hit the man square on the point of his chin. The thud of the punch almost silenced by the sickening crack of the smashed jaw-bone.

The man fell back in agony, knocking Jack and the gunman off their feet. Bogdan ploughed into the group, making straight for the weapon. Two dull thuds rang-out, as the panicked shooter got two rounds off, both missing the Russian and shattering the long mirror beside the door.

Jack was on the leader and had him round the neck, blood, bone and teeth being spit from the man's gasping mouth.

The little thug was no match for the Russian and the sound of Bogdan head-butting the man, rendering him unconscious, heralded the end of the fight.

Jack struggled to keep the younger fitter man in his grip, as Bogdan quickly closed the door. He turned and kicked the leader hard in the stomach. With the wind knocked out of him and the dreadful pain from the jaw wound, the man gave up.

The Russian picked up the revolver just as the shooter came round.

Five or six minutes later, the attackers were tied-up with cords from a couple of bathrobes. Shredded towels were used to secure their feet, and together they lay helpless on the bed.

Blood oozed from the leader's mouth, as the gag was pulled hard around his face.

'I think this fucka is gonna bleed to death, boss.'

'Fuck him,' said Jack. 'Okay, buddy. Go get your gear and get back here A-SAP.'

The Russian turned to the groaning figures on the bed, leaned in close and said, 'Boo!'

Jack grinned and shook his head. 'Get going.'

Jack collected his scattered effects and quickly stuffed them into his bag, then went into the bathroom. He removed his shirt and looked in the mirror. His torso was badly bruised, but he didn't think any ribs were broken. He gently washed the back of his head and winced as he felt the lump. 'Bastard,' he said out loud.

Back in the room he checked the men's restraints, then put on a new shirt, stuffing the blooded and torn one into the waste bin. He looked at his watch, almost 3 o'clock. He found his smartphone, took a photograph of the two thugs, then sat down.

A few minutes later Bogdan knocked at the door. Inside, he said, 'What's the plan, boss?'

Jack turned back to the bed, did a final check, then said, 'We'll leave these boys to enjoy each other's company.'

'Yeah, they probably like that, boss.'

Jack smiled and winked at the two men. 'You ladies have a nice night now. Okay, buddy, we're outta here.'

As he closed the door, Jack hung the DO NOT DISTURB sign on the handle.

Chapter Twenty Six
'Welcome To Serbia'

Not wishing to reveal their destination, Jack politely refused the valet's offer to get them a courtesy car. Instead they walked down into the street and hailed a passing cab.

'Central Railway Station,' said Jack as he climbed in behind his friend.

As the taxi pulled away, Bogdan said quietly, 'What's the plan, boss?'

Jack looked at the driver, then leaned closer to the Russian. 'Someone is definitely onto us, buddy.'

The big man grinned. 'Da, for sure.'

Jack looked at the driver again and continued. 'We need to get the hell outta Montenegro soon as possible, and I don't want to chance the airport. There's a train leaving in twenty-five minutes. I've booked us on it. We'll be across the Serbian border in two hours and into Sarajevo, in two more.'

Bogdan nodded, then leaned back into his seat.

A light rain had started to fall, freshening the muggy atmosphere. For a few minutes there was silence in the back of the cab, then Jack turned to his friend, and said quietly, 'How come you were at the door?'

'What?'

'The suite door. When that fucker opened the door, you were standing there.'

Bogdan grinned. 'Ah, da, okay. When I get to club on roof, there is plenty women. So maybe I have busy

105

night,' the big man winked, 'I think, okay, maybe I miss breakfast. So, I come down to tell you.'

Jack leaned back and smiled . . . 'Thank fuck you did, buddy.' Jack held out the palm of his hand and the Russian slapped it. 'Yeah, thank fuck you did.'

The traffic around the station was congested and the cab had slowed to walking pace. Podgorica Central Station could be seen a hundred yards ahead.

'We'll get out here,' said Jack, as he opened the door.

Bogdan paid the driver and followed his friend. Jack looked at his Rolex. 'We got ten minutes, buddy.'

By the time they got to the station Bogdan was wheezing, clearly not happy with the pace Jack had set.

'You okay, big man?'

The Russian nodded and waved to carry on. The station was busy, and it took a couple of minutes for Jack and Bogdan to get to their platform. The barriers were closing as Jack shouted, 'Hold on, please!'

As they took their seats, the train lurched and pulled out of the station.

The First-Class carriage was not as busy as the rest of the train. Jack smiled and nodded to a lady on the other side of the aisle. 'Just managed to catch it,' he said.

Bogdan had recovered his breath and looked at the woman. 'Nearly kill me.'

She smiled, then continued to tap away on her iPad.

A few minutes later a steward pushing a heavily-laden snack-trolley arrived. 'Would you like a drink, madame?'

She shook her head.

'Gentlemen?'

'Water, please,' said Jack, 'and a Coke.'

'Sir?'

'Water and beer,' said Bogdan.

The two greedily drank the refreshing water, and then sat in silence. It was getting light and the train was almost through the suburbs of the city, the speed and heavy rain blurred the view through the dirty water-streaked windows.

Jack took out his smartphone and swiped the screen. He tapped out a message and attached the photo he took in the banker's study. A second message had the picture of the two thugs attached. He pressed SEND and then leaned back into his seat. He cracked the can of Coke and swallowed half the sweet liquid. Bogdan had already finished his beer and his eyes were closed, ready for sleep.

* * *

It was a few minutes after 3am in London, when Mathew Sterling woke to the sound of his phone, the ping signalling an incoming SMS. He rolled over and took the phone from the bedside table, rubbed his eyes and swiped the screen. A smile appeared as he read Jack's message . . .

3bil (less 3mil) transf equally > Macau Merchant Bank > Azerinternational. Baku > Volks Merchant. Lichtenstein. See attach screenshot. Ends

He opened the next message and the smile disappeared.

107

uninvited guests / cover compromised / now on train to Sarajevo / See attach pic- can u ID? Ends

'Looks like you've stirred up a hornet's nest, big brother,' he said out loud.

* * *

Jack tried to sleep, but the jolting of the train as it rattled over points kept waking him. They'd been traveling for almost two hours and were approaching the border when two Immigration Officials appeared, one from Montenegro, the other from Serbia. Jack watched as they checked and processed the passports of the half-asleep passengers. He shook Bogdan and the big Russian woke with a grunt.

'Passports,' said Jack, nodding to the approaching officials.

'Passports, please,' said the Montenegro official.

Jack handed his over and watched as the guy flicked through the pages, nodded and stamped the document.

Bogdan's was processed in the same casual manner and both were handed over to the Serbian officer. 'You are travelling to where?'

'Sarajevo,' said Jack, with a smile. 'We'll take a flight from there back to Moscow.'

'Why not fly from Podgorica?'

'My friend here likes trains.'

The official looked at the Russian. Bogdan smiled, and raised his hand as if pulling a cord, 'Choo-choo! Choo-choo!'

The official stared at the big man for several seconds, a puzzled look on his face, then stamped the passports and slid them across the table. 'Welcome to Serbia.'

They crossed the border right on schedule, an announcement in Montenegrin, Serbian and English, declaring the fact.

Jack smiled at the woman across from them. 'You travelling to Sarajevo too?'

She smiled back. 'Yes I travel. My English not good . . . sorry.'

Jack continued to smile. 'Well you understood me, so I guess it's not that bad.'

'I understand some . . . I speak some, thank you.'

'Very good,' said Jack nodding.

She placed her iPad on the table and Jack noticed a news headline on the screen. Pointing to the tablet, he said, 'May I see that please?'

The woman handed him the device and said, 'Yes, please.'

Bogdan was trying to sleep, but Jack nudged him awake.

'Da?'

'Can you read this?'

The big man took the tablet and looked at the screen. There was a picture of Silvio Schlovan and Esther, dressed in evening attire, at some function or other, probably a stock photo the news media had. Below the picture were headlines and a short report in Montenegrin.

'Well?' said Jack.'

Bogdan leaned closer, and said quietly, 'They dead, boss.'

'Can you read more?'

'Not well. But says there was intruder. And were killed.'

Jack took the iPad and passed it back to the woman. 'Thank you.' He turned to Bogdan, and said under his breath, 'Fuck. We've stirred up a hornet's nest.'

Chapter Twenty Seven
'Strange Message'

Jack's father-in-law, Dimitri Mikhailovich Orlov, was a true Russian oligarch in every sense of the word. He'd made billions from oil, mining and steel, and held a large portfolio of extremely lucrative properties in all the major cities. As a hobby he owned a premier league football club in the north of England, but his pride and joy, after his own beloved 'Orel Island' off the coast of Abu Dhabi, was his prestigious golf club in Scotland.

All this of course paled into insignificance, when it came to his beautiful daughter Nicole and his two granddaughters.

Dimitri, or Mitri, as he was known to family and close friends, was at home, on Orel.

A well-known and respected figure within the international world of finance, he was a tough strong-willed negotiator. In his private life, generous to a fault.

A major factor in his success was his intelligence network. 'Information is power' was his favourite quote, and his network was legend. It was said, he had more contacts across the world than the CIA, especially in the Former Soviet Union.

Orlov was at the big desk that reputedly once belonged to Winston Churchill when Olga, his long-standing PA, entered. 'Excuse me, Mitri.' the informality was accepted and expected when they were alone. 'There's been a strange message.'

The old man looked up and smiled. 'Really? Something interesting I hope?'

Olga placed a leather folder on the desk. Dimitri put on his spectacles and picked up a print-out of a photograph. 'That's Jack. Looks to be in a railway station.'

'Yes, and I think the man with him, is a friend of his from Moscow.'

The old man squinted slightly. 'Yes, Bogdan, Bogdan Markov.'

Olga tapped the other sheet in the folder. 'This is a printout of the message that came with the photograph.'

Your son-in-law does not know what he is involved in. British Intelligence has put him at great risk. We are your friends Orlov. We wish to help you and him.

Mitri looked up. 'Where was the picture taken?'

Olga took the paper and pointed to a sign a few yards behind Jack. Again, he squinted. 'PODGORICA . . . That's Montenegro.'

'Da.'

'How did we get this?'

'Came into my company email.'

Orlov stood and went to the big windows and looked out over the shimmering waters of the Arabian Gulf. After several seconds he turned and said, 'You think this is genuine, Olga?'

'I can't see any benefit to them if it isn't. They don't ask for anything. They say they wish to help. But with what?'

112

He looked at the message again. Before he could speak, she picked up his smartphone and handed it to him.

He smiled, 'Thank you, darling.'

Chapter Twenty Eight
'Mixed Messages'

As the train passed through the outskirts of Sarajevo, Jack watched as the still ruined and burnt out buildings, flashed past, the legacy from one of the most brutal conflicts in modern history. Jack thought he saw the slightest of tears in his friend's eyes, as he too took in the derelict and forgotten home-ships.

'Back in the badlands, buddy.'

The big man nodded and said nothing.

'Lost friends?'

Bogdan nodded again in silence.

Jack's smartphone beeped, breaking into the pair's reveries. He swiped the screen and said, 'Mitri. How are you? Everything okay?'

'Hello, my boy. I'm fine, everything's fine with me. How about you?'

Bogdan saw the puzzled look on his friend's face.

'Whatsup, Mitri?'

'Where are you, Jack?'

'We're just coming into Sarajevo. Why, what is it, sir?

'We've received a rather cryptic message.'

'Okay? About what?'

'You, Jack.'

Jack frowned. 'Saying what?'

'Olga's forwarding it to your phone as we speak.'

'Okay, hold on please.'

Bogdan said quietly, 'Problem?'

Jack shrugged, as his smartphone pinged the incoming message. He opened the photo, then turned the screen to Bogdan. Jack read the message, and it too was shown to his friend.

'Where did you get this, Mitri?'

'Came into Olga's company email.'

'Okay. Can't really talk here, we're still on the train. I'll call you back when we get someplace a little more private, sir.'

'Very well. Take care, my boy.'

Sarajevo Central looks more like an old-fashioned airport terminal, than a rail station. Built in the 70's by the Former Soviet Union and, with its curved central structure and high arched roof, speaks to an era long gone. Nowadays, this rather large edifice is far too big for the number of trains it services.

Their train pulled into the unwelcoming platform and Jack and Bogdan disembarked with the rest of the arriving passengers. The weather was warm and pleasant, and the morning sun shone in a cloudless sky. They made their way to the exit and across the large square at the front of the terminal.

'There,' said Bogdan, pointing to a small hotel on the far side of the main road.

Jack nodded, and they headed for the hostelry.

The interior had been modernised and was far more hospitable than the exterior would suggest. At the rear was a large garden area, which was set out as a restaurant and currently serving breakfast.

'This'll do, buddy,' said Jack

'Da,' said the big man, 'I'm starving.'

They took a table in the corner, under the shade of a small olive tree.

In broken English, a young woman bid them good morning, then, pointing to a small service counter, said, 'Please help to buffet. I bring tea coffee?'

'Tea, please. Two,' said Jack, showing two fingers to ensure understanding.

The woman smiled and left.

'You gonna eat, boss?'

'Yeah, in a minute, buddy. I'll call Dimitri first. You go ahead.'

The phone rang once. 'Jack.'

'Mitri, Hello again, sir.'

'What are you up to over there, Jack?'

'Can't say too much, sir. This line is not totally secure.'

'I understand. So, what do you think about the message?'

Jack paused for a few seconds, then said, 'I had some unwelcome guest in my room last night.'

'Are you okay, my boy?'

'A few bruises and a sore head, but nothing serious.'

'I don't know why you still get involved with this kind of thing, Jack.?'

'With respect, Mitri, now's not the time.'

'No, of course. You were saying?'

'Just a second, sir.' Jack waited as the woman left the tea-pot. He nodded thanks and put the phone back to his ear. 'So I guess we were being watched, but by whom?

The message was not threatening, so maybe they do wish to help? But who are they?'

'I've been thinking about that, Jack. Olga managed to source the origin of the email. She tells me the IP address was somewhere in Italy. Most likely Florence.'

'Okay. Not sure what that means, Mitri.'

'I think I might. Can you give me an hour or so?'

'Yes, of course.'

'Good. Sit tight and I'll get back to you.'

'Will do. Thank you Mitri. Oh, and, sir.'

'Yes?'

'No mention of this if you're speaking to Nicole.'

'No, of course not, my boy.'

The line went silent.

Bogdan returned with a large plate piled high with cheese, smoked sausage, olives, boiled eggs and bread. A second plate held half a dozen Danish pastries.

Jack grinned. 'A bit peckish are we, big man?'

Bogdan took his seat and poured some tea. 'Da.'

Jack poured some tea and helped himself to one of the pastries. Bogdan looked like he was about to cry. 'Calm down I'll go and get some more.'

The Russian grinned as he loaded cheese and sausage onto a thick slice of crusty bread.

'What did Orlov say?'

'He's gonna make some enquires, getting back to us. We'll sit it out here before we make our next move.'

Bogdan nodded as he chomped away on his food.

Jack swiped his smartphone screen and waited. 'Jack.'

'Good morning. darling.'

'You ok, Zaikin?'

'I'm fine babe. How's the girls.'

'Playing up this morning. Svetlana is having trouble getting them ready. And I have to go into London for a meeting.'

Jack smiled. 'Svetlana's been their nanny since the day they were born, babe. She'll cope.'

'Where are you, darling?'

'Still in the Balkans. Moving on soon.'

'To where?'

'Not sure yet but I'll stay in touch.'

'Okay. Be careful, Zaikin. I love you.'

'Love you too Nikki. Kiss the twins.'

'Okay, bye.'

He tapped out a message and then made a second call.

'Jack. Good morning.'

'Morning Matt. How y'doin?'

'Fine, but what about you? You okay?'

'Yeah, okay. Few bruises, a sore head.'

'What's this you've just sent, Jack?'

'That picture and message was sent to Dimitri.'

'From whom?'

'Dimitri's working on that as we speak.'

'Right.' The line went quiet . . .

'Matt?'

'Yes, Jack. Okay, I think you should get back here for the moment. You've discovered where the funds went, so there's a good chance the government can get them back. Or at least most of it.'

'It's your call, Mathew. You're the boss. But let's wait and see what Dimitri comes up with first, eh?'

118

'Fair enough. You secure for the moment?'

'Sure. We're sitting in the sunshine having breakfast. Bogdan thinks he's on holiday.'

Mathew laughed. 'How's he doing?'

'He's good. Saved my arse last night.'

'Give him my regards.'

'Talking about last night, we saw on the news that Silvio Schlovan and his wife were murdered.'

'Jesus, Jack. That's it, get back here.'

'Calm down, bro.'

'Don't you see, Jack? To all intents and purposes, you were the last to see them alive. It could look like you killed them.'

'Never thought of that. Thought they'd been killed because he gave us information. Was surprised how fast he was taken out though.'

The line was silent again . . .

'Mathew?'

'Yes, I'm here. The bank must have a ghost server somewhere.'

'Ghost server? What the hell's that?'

'It's a duplicate server that monitors every transaction, every log-in, anything that has gone through the bank's server is mirrored on the ghost server.'

'Right, like a Big-Brother overwatch.'

'Yes. With operatives monitoring 24/7.'

'Silvio must have known they would be able to see what he was doing.'

'Yes. And they killed him for it, Jack.'

Chapter Twenty Nine
'We Go To Italy'

It was almost an hour and a half later when Dimitri called.

'Jack, my boy. Sorry to be so long.'

Jack grinned. 90 minutes to come up with information, that would normally take a week to discover. 'No problem, sir. What you got?'

'I'm going to have Olga send you something. Should be helpful.'

'Thank you, Mitri.'

'No problem, Jack. But please, be very careful.'

'Always, sir. Thank you.'

The line went silent.

A few minutes later his smartphone pinged an incoming message. Jack read through Dimitri's information with surprise and disbelief.

Bogdan watched as his friend scrolled through the message. 'Okay, boss?'

Jack nodded, and continued to read, then sat back and slid his chair further under the shade of the olive tree. He passed the phone to Bogdan.

'Can this be true, boss?'

'Seems farfetched, I agree. But Dimitri's not one for passing on rubbish. His intelligence is usually correct.'

Bogdan slid the phone across the table. 'So, what's the plan now.'

'I'm sending this to London. See what Mathew thinks.'

The waitress returned. 'You want more tea?'

Jack looked at his Rolex, almost 10:30. They'd been there over two hours, and three pots of tea. The breakfast buffet had been cleared and they were the only ones in the garden.'

'Can I have a Coke, please?'

She smiled. 'Yes please.'

'More tea,' said Bogdan.

Jack had just finished the Coke when his phone beeped. He swiped the screen. 'Mathew.'

'Jack, hello.'

'So, what d'you think?'

'To be honest, Jack, nothing much surprises me anymore. And this could be what we need.'

'Might also be a trap?'

'If they wanted to kill you, they could have done that in Podgorica.'

'Don't forget the two muppets in the hotel, Matt. Did you get any ID on them?'

'No. We have nothing yet, and Interpol hasn't got back to us. But I think they're more likely to be from the bank.'

'Why?'

'You said they wanted to know who you worked for?'

'Yeah.'

'Based on the message to Dimitri, the people following you clearly knew that.'

'Right. So, the jokers in the hotel were just part of the bank's heavy-mob. Low down on the food-chain?'

'I think so, Jack.'

'Okay. I guess our next move is obvious.'

'I'll have Victoria arrange flights. Get to the airport and she'll send you the details.'

'Okay, bro. If nothing else, it'll get us outta the Balkans.'

'Right. Talk soon. Be safe, Jack.'

'Cheers Matt.'

The line went silent.

Jack stood up and stretched the muscles in his back. 'Get the bill, buddy, and don't be mean with the tip.'

The big Russian smiled. 'So, we go to Italy, boss?'

'Da, Bogdan. We go to Italy.'

The original Sarajevo International was built in the 60's with funding from the Former Soviet Union. Nowadays, with the volume of international flights, it is no longer fit-for-purpose, and a massive upgrade and expansion is currently underway.

The taxi from the hotel to the airport took less than ten minutes, but with all the construction traffic around the developing terminal, it took twice as long to get into Departures.

Jack and Bogdan made their way to the Austrian Airways ticket desk, as AA was the first flight Mathew's PA, could arrange. The good news was, the flight departed at 2pm. with no delays expected. The not-so-good news was, it was via Vienna, where they had a four-hour layover, with an expected time of arrival into

Peretola International at nine that evening. All that notwithstanding, Jack was not too unhappy about spending a night or two in Florence. He just wished Nicole was with him.

Chapter Thirty
'Borgo San Lorenzo'

The flight, as expected, did depart on time and the layover in the Business Lounge in Vienna was not unpleasant. Bogdan ate, and drank a few beers, then drifted off to sleep in the comfy armchair. Jack spent over half an hour chatting to Nicole and his daughters, who were delighted to hear daddy's voice.

A short call to Mathew to 'check-in' and see if there were any up-dates, was followed by an unexpected call from Dimitri.

'Hello, my boy.'

'Hello, sir. Whatsup?'

'I have a little more information for you. Might save you some time in Florence.'

'Okay, thanks, Mitri.'

'Olga will send you a location shortly. I've spoken with them and they are expecting you tonight.'

'Right . . . we don't land until twenty-one-hundred hours. So, depending on where the place is, we could be late.'

'It's not an issue, Jack. They'll be there waiting for you.'

'Sounds good. Thank you, sir.'

'And, Jack . . . please be careful. These are extremely powerful people you are dealing with.'

The second leg of their journey also went as hoped, with the plane touching down at Peretola International a few minutes before 9pm. Jack had googled the location Olga had sent, about twelve miles north-east of Florence, close to the small town of Borgo San Lorenzo.

They cleared Immigration and Customs and made their way to the waiting line of taxis. The driver, clearly happy to pick-up two visitors, had the thought of making a little extra money on the fare, but when Jack gave the destination in perfect Italian, the driver shrugged and pulled away from the kerb.

The ride from the airport to San Lorenzo took a little over forty-five minutes, and although the town was only twelve miles from Florence, as-the-crow-flies, it was almost thirty miles by road. Once there it took a few more minutes to find the actual location, and when the cab pulled up to the gates, the driver was clearly apprehensive, as there was nothing but darkness.

The sky was black, with the moon obscured behind heavy cloud. As the gates swung silently open two figures emerged from the shadows. One stood in front of the car, the headlights glinting on the Beretta machine-pistol in his hands. The second, opened the rear door and said, 'Buona sera, signiori.'

Jack paid the driver and climbed out. 'Buona sera.'

The man then turned to the driver, and with a wave of his hand, said, 'Avanti.'

As the taxi pulled away, the man indicated a six-seater golf buggy, just to the right of the gate. 'Prego, signiori.'

Jack and Bogdan took the middle seats, as the man with the gun sat behind them. The cart lurched as it pulled away into the shadows. They continued for a couple of minutes through a heavily wooded area and then came out onto a well-lit driveway. A hundred yards ahead, and surrounded by floodlit gardens, was what appeared to be a 12th century castle.

As the buggy pulled up to the bottom of the entrance steps, a man, dressed in evening suit, came down to greet them. Jack and Bogdan climbed out, and the cart drove off.

The man offered his hand. 'Good evening, Mr Castle.'

As they shook hands, Jack said, 'Good evening. This is . . . '

'Mr Markov. Yes, we are expecting you both.' He offered his hand to Bogdan.

The big Russian smiled. 'Hullo.'

'My name is Giovanni. Welcome to the Castello San Lorenzo, gentlemen.'

Jack and Bogdan followed Giovanni into the old building. The exterior, although well maintained, was as it had been, almost a thousand years ago. The interior had kept its medieval countenance, but it was clear the castle had been modernised with state of the art air-conditioning, new marble floors and contemporary windows. The walls were hung with works by many of the old masters and the statues were an equal to any in the museums of Florence or Rome. Antique furniture was everywhere. This was not contrived opulence, this was the real deal.

Giovanna said, 'Here we are,' then turned and opened a heavily-studded oak door.

As they entered the room the occupants stood to greet them. Two men and a woman, probably between sixty and seventy, dressed elegantly in evening-wear, stood in front of a huge fireplace.

'Gentlemen, please come in,' said the woman.

Giovanni introduced Jack and Bogdan to the woman. This is the Contessa Maria Alaria di Vincenzo.'

'Contessa,' said Jack, as he took her hand and kissed it.

The woman smiled. 'Please, call me Maria. And, Mr Markov. Welcome.'

The Russian smiled.

Maria introduced the other men. 'This is my great friend Myles DeVere, one of your fellow countrymen, Jack. And this is Takashi Miori, recently arrived from Japan.'

Hands were shaken, and they sat down on the three large chesterfields that surrounded a low coffee table. A silver ice bucket with an unopened bottle of vintage Dom Perignon, a couple of decanters of spirit and several small bottles of mineral water where laid out.

'Can we get you a drink gentleman,' said Giovanni.

'Water's fine, thank you,'

The woman smiled. 'Yes of course. You don't drink, do you, Jack. Not so you, Mr Bogdan?'

The big man smiled. 'Da. Not so me, Contessa.'

Chapter Thirty One
'Templari Incrementum'

Early in the 12th century the French knight, Hugues de Payens founded the original order of Knights Templar. For almost 200 years the Templars grew in numbers, wealth and power, and their contribution to the Crusades was legend.

Not by accident, did the Templars develop into what would be known today as a multi-international corporation, with interest in banking, investments and the wider control of wealth, across the civilised world. Their links to Freemasonry and even the Illuminati, did nothing but strengthen their position.

As the Templar's influence grew, it became clear King Phillipe 4th of France was in fear of their power and hold on the world of finance; this, plus the fact he was personally in crippling debt to them. To free himself from their grip, he initiated vile rumours that the Templars were nothing more than money-grabbing devil-worshipping Heretics.

On Friday 13th October 1307, Templars across Europe were simultaneously arrested, tortured and put to death. This action by Phillipe, was designed to deliver three goals. The first, get rid of his debt. The second, get rid of the Templars. The third, secure their vast wealth. The first two were achieved, not so the third, and although huge amounts of monies were seized, most of the Knights Templar fortune remained undiscovered.

Over the centuries, and to the present day, the original Templar fortune has grown and grown. It is a closely guarded secret just how much money is now in the hands of the descendants of the Knights Templar, and today, with their unlimited funding, they can direct world events, influence governments and control almost any situation.

It is believed there are about six hundred direct progenies of the original Templars, and although they are spread across the world, their High Council is based, and meets in Florence. Today, these descendants are known as, Templari Incrementum.

The Contessa Maria Alaria di Vincenzo, is the current Grand Master of the Templari, and head of the Council of Thirteen. This number of male and female council members, in reverence to the dreadful date their ancestors perished.

'You are a very resourceful man, Jack,' said the Contessa.

Jack finished his water and looked at the woman. 'Not as resourceful as your organisation though, Contessa.'

She smiled. 'Maria, please. Well, we have been established for almost a millennium, Jack.'

He nodded. 'There is that, I suppose. May I ask a question, Contessa . . . Maria?'

'Your organisation has been following us. Why? What makes us so interesting? And why are you so obviously willing to help us?'

'Ah, the directness of the British. I do so like it. So, we come to the business of the evening,' she waved her hand and said, 'Giovanni, prego.'

'Si, Contessa.' The man took a stance in front of the huge fireplace, as if about to deliver a dramatic speech. Jack looked at Bogdan who was clearly supressing a grin.

'We know of the recent and unfortunate Poseidon incident. We know your government paid three billion pounds to the high-jackers. We also know you have been tasked with recovering the money and finding the person or persons responsible.'

Jack picked up another bottle of water and poured it into the crystal tumbler, then looked across at DeVere. The Englishman raised his glass in a knowing gesture and smiled.

'You traced the money,' continued Giovanni, 'thanks to your good friend Mr Bogdan here to the Henagar Bank, and have established the onward transactions.'

'With respect, Giovanni, we know all this,' said Jack.

'Please . . . Jack,' said the woman. 'We are coming to the point,' she raised her hand in an elegant gesture and said, 'Giovanni.'

'Si, grazie, Contessa. What you have yet to discover, is who the responsible people are.'

'And you're about to tell us?'

Giovanni, with a look of mild annoyance at the interruption, put his shoulders back and continued. 'The Templari are, at their core, the descendants of the original Templars, as I am sure your father-in-law, Dimitri Mikhailovich Orlov, has told you?'

Jack nodded, unsurprised that Mitri would know of the existence of such an organisation.

'That said, it is not unusual for us to allow, on occasion, outsiders, shall we say, into our organisation. This of course is subject to the strictest criteria.'

'Which is?'

The annoyed look returned. 'That, I'm afraid I cannot go into, Jack. With one exception. The final requirement, for an outsider, is the ability to contribute to the organisation financially.'

Jack nodded.

'The individual seeking affiliation with the Templari, must contribute two billion dollars.'

'Wow,' said Jack, 'that's me out then.'

'Not so your father-in- law, Jack,' said Takashi.

'Ah . . . You know Dimitri?'

'I do, Jack. And I am honoured to say we are now friends.'

'Friends?'

'Yes. For the last three years we have been negotiating the sale of my steel company.'

Jack nodded and smiled. 'Right. So that's how we came to be here.'

'Gentlemen,' said Giovanni, 'we are getting a little off-piste.'

Takashi bowed his head slightly. 'Excuse me.'

'We have recently been approached by one such outsider.' Giovanni turned and took a fine leather folder from the broad mantle. Passing it to Jack, he said, 'This is the man who seeks to join us. This is also the man who, we believe is responsible for the Poseidon incident.'

Jack opened the folder and looked at the photograph, then passed it to Bogdan, who shook his head and handed it back.

'Who is he, Giovanni?'

'He is prone to using an alias, but now he goes by the rather colourful name of Mr Rick Washington. He has had extensive facial reconstruction to hide his real identity of course.'

'Which is?'

Giovanni smiled. 'I believe you know him as Greg Stoneham.'

Chapter Thirty Two
'Good Morning'

It was a little after 6am. when Jack woke from a deep sleep. For a second or two he didn't know where he was. As his eyes adjusted to the sunshine coming through the French window, he stretched the muscles in his back and sat up. He went to the window, opened it and stepped out onto the small balcony. The view from the rear of the castle was more spectacular than the imposing front. A large lake, that fed a moat to three sides of the castle, sparkled in the warm Tuscan sun. The delightful sound of the dawn-chorus filled the air, then the crunch of horse's hooves, on the immaculate gravel, made him look to the left. A large black stallion trotted towards the lake. Contessa Maria Alaria di Vincenzo, in full riding habit, sat astride the magnificent animal. She looked up and waved her crop, 'Good morning, Jack.'

He returned the wave. 'Good morning, Maria'

'Would you care to join me?'

'Not right now. But thank you.'

The woman's smile lit up her face. 'Perhaps when you're dressed?'

It was then Jack realised, he was on the balcony naked.

Before leaving his room, he tapped out a message to Mathew, briefing him on the previous evening's events and revelations, then attached the photograph. Rick

Washington's mug-shot would soon be circulated to the CIA and Interpol.

It hadn't surprised Jack to discover it was his old adversary, Greg Stoneham, behind the hi-jacking. The DNA on Sir Anthony Grainger's body matched the ex-CIA agent's, and Stoneham's arrogance, and confidence in his new appearance, would not have worried him about leaving a trace. The surgery he'd undergone on his face, was indeed extensive, and it would be almost impossible for anyone to recognise the original Stoneham. Even, according to Giovanni, the man's limp had gone.

Questions raced through Jack's mind. *Why would Washington want to join the Templari? It was clear why he wanted the three billion, to buy his way in and then maintain the lifestyle. But why this organisation? Did he think if he became part of this all powerful society he would become not only invisible but untouchable? Or was there more to the Templari, than met the eye?*

At 8am Jack joined Myles, Takashi and Giovanni in the dining room. Bogdan had eaten earlier and taken himself off to the sauna. The Contessa was still out riding.

'Good morning, gentlemen,' said Jack, as he took a seat at the table.

Responses came from each in turn.

'Please, Jack,' said Giovanni, as he pointed to a large Louis Quatorze sideboard. 'Help yourself to breakfast. Tea and coffee are here.'

Jack poured some tea, and said, 'Thank you,' then turned to Takashi. 'So, you and Dimitri are friends?'

The oriental wiped his mouth with a linen napkin. 'Indeed, we are. As I said last evening, I am honoured to be so.'

'So, I would be correct in saying it was you who sent the initial email to him?'

Takashi inclined his head in a polite manner. 'Not me personally, but I was instrumental in making the contact. Especially when we discovered you were related to Dimitri.'

Jack sipped at the hot tea. 'So, you knew who I was, and what we were doing.'

'Our organisation did. Yes.'

Jack looked DeVere in the eyes. 'And that information could only have come from the British Security Service.'

The Englishman smiled. 'Our intelligence network is second to none, Jack. We collect information from all over the world and, when required, intervene.'

Jack didn't like the man, even if he was a Brit. Pompous, arrogant and privileged, was the description that came to mind. 'And who decides when you . . . intervene?'

'The council, Jack. No one person can make any decision. The council acts on behalf of the organisation and the organisation, for the betterment of the world as a whole.'

'Wow,' said Jack, 'that's a pretty sweeping statement, Myles. Sounds a bit all powerful and God-like, don't you think?'

Takashi sensed the tension between the two Englishmen. 'Not God-like Jack. And we are not about power.'

Jack looked at the mild mannered Asian. 'Really? Then what?'

'Order. We bring order where it is needed. There is nothing sinister about us, Jack. Secretive, yes. But sinister, certainly not.'

The door opened, and the Contessa entered. 'Gentlemen, good morning,' then touching Jack gently on the shoulder, she smiled. 'And good morning again to you, Mr Castle.'

He returned the smile. 'Maria.'

She went to the sideboard, helped herself to a plate of scrambled eggs and smoked salmon, then returned and sat opposite Jack. 'Will you be staying with us a little longer, Jack. Or will you be leaving us today?'

'As much as I'd love to enjoy more of your hospitality, Maria, we really do need to go. And too much luxury is bad for Bogdan.'

'As you wish. Giovanni will see that you get back to Florence.'

'Thank you. You've been very kind.'

An hour later, at the front of the castle, Jack and Bogdan shook hands with Takashi and Giovanni. DeVere was conspicuous by his absence. Jack turned to the woman and shook her hand gently. 'It was a great pleasure to meet you, Contessa.'

She smiled. 'And you. Perhaps we'll meet again but, in the meantime, be careful, Mr Castle.'

Jack returned the smile. 'Always.'

They climbed into the waiting Bentley and the chauffeur closed the door. As the car pulled away, Jack looked up to the window above and saw the face of Myles DeVere looking down.

Chapter Thirty Three
'Disappointing'

The cool wind off the Mediterranean made the heat from the sun bearable. The villa on the hilltop, above Monte Carlo, was small but luxurious. Rick Washington floated effortlessly in the infinity pool, the sunlight sparkling on the water. He was happy. His plan to extort the massive ransom from the British had worked better than he'd ever imagined. And now, anyone who had been involved was dead.

Even his illustrious partner, Sir Anthony Grainger, had contributed far more than expected. Abducting his own family was a master stroke, obviously to protect his own neck and deflect any involvement from himself, but still a stroke of genius.

It was a pity the man hadn't died on the pavement in Knightsbridge and had to be dispatched in hospital. But even that amused Washington. He smiled to himself as he recalled the feeling, the assassin's tingle, when you kill with your bare hands.

But all that was behind him. Now he would become respectable, and able to live his life in luxurious anonymity. The admission to the Templari Incrementum would ensure that. He had only to wait for their call. Then, after transferring the two billion, he would be untouchable.

The two men they had watching him were useless. He'd spotted them as soon as he boarded the train from Florence and, although they alternated their surveillance, they were still easy to spot. It didn't worry him. He knew the Templari would watch him, but he also knew they were only interested in his ability to come up with the money. *Fuck them*, he thought to himself.

He looked across at the woman next to the pool. He smiled. She'd nearly killed him the night before. 'Hey, baby. Can you bring me a beer, please?'

She slowly stood up, her bare breasts and torso glistening with oil. He watched her glide into the villa. 'What an ass,' he said out-loud.

She looked over her shoulder and winked, then disappeared inside.

It was late afternoon when the call came. 'Giovanni, so good to hear from you,' said Washington.

'Mr Washington. Yes, yes, nice to speak to you too.'

'Please, Giovanni, call me Rick.'

'Yes of course . . . Rick. Well I'm sure you know why I am calling.'

'I do indeed.'

Giovanni could hear the excitement in the American's voice. 'I'm afraid I have some disappointing news, Mr Washing . . . Rick.'

'Disappointing?'

'Yes. The council has carefully considered your petition, but I'm sorry to say they are not able to approve your request at this time.'

'What? I don't understand. I have the two billion. I can transfer it immediately. Today.'

'It is not just about the money, Rick.'

'You're shittin me! It's always about the money, with people like you.'

'Please, Mr Washington, there is no need . . .'
'Fuck you and fuck the rest of those assholes.'
The line went silent.

Washington went out to the patio. He looked down the hill to the beautiful harbour and the billions of dollars worth of yachts in the marina. His heart was pounding, his breath came hard and fast. He turned to the woman, still lying out in the sun, and said quietly, 'Get out.'

She slid the designer sunglasses down her nose and looked over the rim. 'What?'

He raised his voice. 'I said get out.'

'But we . . .'

'Get your fuckin ass outta here,' he screamed.

The woman jumped up and ran into the villa. A few minutes later he heard her shout, 'Asshole,' and the front door slam shut.

The two Templari had seen the woman leave over an hour before. Now they watched as Rick Washington drove out from the villa gates. The sleek Audi R8, the roof down, accelerated away and up the hill. They quickly started their engine and slipped onto the road, a hundred yards behind the fast moving vehicle. The winding road took them to the summit, over the top and down the other side, into the woods north of Monte Carlo. The agents followed. The Audi was moving fast, and they had to work hard to keep up. Then, as they turned a bend in the road, there it was, pulled into a lay-by under a large olive tree. They stopped the car about twenty yards away.

There was no sign of Washington. They got out as the sun was setting. The shadows in the woods made it difficult to see into the semi darkness. They moved slowly towards the parked Audi.

'Stand still.'

The men stopped.

'Turn around . . . slowly.'

They turned to face Washington, the hunters now the hunted. He smiled. 'You fuckin amateurs.' In his hand was a Glock automatic, fitted with a snub-nose silencer. 'Into the woods ladies . . . Move it.'

The two men looked at each other, then began walking into the shadow.

Chapter Thirty Four
'Avenue des Anglais'

The return journey to Peretola International, was decidedly more comfortable than their previous taxi ride. The sleek Bentley pulled up to the departures area and the chauffeur bid them a safe journey.

Peretola, although classed as international, is not that big an airport, so Jack and Bogdan had to fly via Rome before travelling on to the South of France. The Alitalia flight from Peretola to Rome was busy, but not so the onward leg to Nice.

It was a little after 6pm when the wheels bounced onto the tarmac and, as the plane taxied towards the terminal, Jack made a quick call to Nicole. 'You okay, Zaikin?'

'I'm fine, darling. How you doin?'

'We're all good here. Where are you, Jack?'

'Just landed in the South of France.'

'The Cote d'Azur?'

'Yeah, babe.'

'Lucky you!'

'It's just work, darling.'

He heard her chuckle. 'Yeah right, mister.'

'Okay, baby, gotta go, just wanted to check-in.'

'Be careful, Jack. Love you.'

'Love you too. Kiss the girls.'

The line went silent.

After quickly clearing Immigration and Customs, they rented a car from one of the more reputable agencies. Bogdan was adamant he did not want a 'little' Jaguar.

With an unhappy frown, he said, 'I can't get in those fuckin things, boss.'

So, when Jack tossed him the keys to a Range Rover, the smile returned to the big man's face.

The Russian pulled out of the parking area and onto the main road. Jack had tapped the location of Washington's villa into the Sat-Nav, the display read 32 miles and 45 minutes. It directed them onto the main coast road east, along the Avenue des Anglais and through Nice, on to Villefranche and Beaulieu-sur-Mer, then finally into Monaco.

Jack knew the area well. He and Nicole holidayed here a lot, staying at their villa in Cap Ferrat. The Avenue des Anglais was busy and the sidewalks bustled with happy tourists from all over the world. The slow moving traffic was peppered with some of the most expensive cars available.

As they passed the Hotel Negresco, Jack smiled.

'Why you smile, boss?'

Jack pointed to the elegant hotel. 'That hotel, the Negresco. Nikki and I had one of the best meals of our lives there.'

'Looks expensive, boss.'

Jack nodded. 'Yeah, kind of.'

A gaudily illuminated pedal-taxi swerved in front of them, the Russian hit the horn hard. 'Stukah,' he shouted out the window. 'What the fuck is that?'

'They're just modern-day rickshaws, big man.'

'Rickshaw belongs in fuckin China, boss, not here.
Jack laughed.

'What is plan when we get there?'

'We'll play it by ear.'

'Play it with ear? What is this?'

Jack laughed. 'We'll decide once we see the situation.'

'Okay, da. But we have no weapons. This guy will be armed for sure.'

Jack put his hand on his friend's shoulder and smiled. 'Yes. But I have you, big man.'

Bogdan turned to Jack. 'You are real bullshitter, boss.'

They both laughed.

It was almost eight o'clock when the Sat-Nav declared, 'You have arrived at your destination.'

They parked the Range Rover a good hundred yards from the gates of the villa and got out. It was quiet, with only the odd vehicle passing, the moon offered some light to the dark roadway. They walked in silence.

Twenty yards from the gates they stopped, and Jack said quietly, 'I'll go over the wall. You go down the hill here, see if you can see anything from the back.'

'Da, okay, boss.'

'We just check it out first. Don't go in. Not until we see what we're dealing with.'

'Niet problem.'

Jack waited a few moments as his friend crept down the hill. The lights from the sparkling marina, three miles below, did nothing to illuminate the hillside, and within seconds the big Russian disappeared into the darkness.

Jack made his way to the wall and pulled himself up. The short driveway and gardens were all lit up but, from his viewpoint, the villa looked to be in darkness. He waited a few more seconds then heaved himself over the wall, dropping down behind a large bougainvillea. Again, he waited and listened. Nothing. There was no vehicle in the drive but that didn't mean anything. Moving slowly and keeping to what shadow there was in the illuminated garden, he approached the building. He looked through the windows. The villa was in darkness.

He could see right the way through to the rear of the property and out to the pool area, then he heard the sound. He quickly bent down and picked up a large ornamental owl. He felt the weight of it in his hand, then raised it high, ready for anything.

'You there, boss?' said the big man, as he came around the corner of the house.

'Here, buddy.'

'Place is deserted, boss.'

'Yeah.'

Bogdan pointed to the owl. 'What's that?'

Jack grinned. 'Oh, just doing a bit of bird-watchin,' then put the ornament back in place.

'Front or back?' said Bogdan.

'In the back, buddy.'

They moved to the rear of the property and found one of the smaller windows unlocked. Jack struggled in, and a few moments later appeared at the big patio doors. He slid them open and said, 'Check the place over. There's bound to be weapons here.'

145

Chapter Thirty Five
'Intruder'

Washington got back to the edge of the woods, about fifty yards away from his car. He stood in the shadows and waited a few minutes to be sure there was nothing on the road. Happy he was alone, he came out and jogged quickly to the lay-by. He looked up and down the road again, and was about to climb in, when he saw the parked VW.

'Fuck,' he said out loud.

He ran to the car and smiled when he saw the keys in the ignition. Quickly he drove up over the grassy verge and through the trees, bumping into several as he found a way in. By weaving in and out he managed to get the vehicle well away from the road.

It'd be impossible to see at night, but even in daylight it would not be found unless someone stumbled across it. He switched off the engine, wiped his prints from the door handles and steering wheel, then threw the keys away into the darkness. A few minutes later he was back in the Audi and heading to the villa. He was at the crest of the hill when his smartphone pinged several times. He looked at the screen . . . INTRUDER.

He stopped the car, swiped the screen and tapped the security application. It showed the patio doors had been opened. 'What the fuck,' he said out loud.

He thought for several seconds, his mind racing. *It can't be the Templari already. Burglars maybe. Yeah, it had to be. There were always thefts from the villas.* He grinned and set off down the hill.

A few minutes later he pulled to the side of the road and parked. He waited and watched as the odd car came and went, each time illuminating the gates of his villa. There was a big 4x4 parked on the other side of the road. That meant two to five men. He took out a small pair of binoculars. No one in the truck. *That's an expensive vehicle for burglars,* he thought.

He was about to drive away, then remembered the four hundred thousand dollars in the concealed floor-safe. *Is it worth the risk?* he thought.

He checked the Glock, a full magazine less four rounds. *Is it worth it. Do I really need four hundred K?*

He looked at the 4x4 again, smiled, then started the engine. 'Au revoir, Monaco,' he said out loud.

Chapter Thirty Six
'Every Eight Hours'

The sun was coming up over the bay. Bogdan had fallen asleep, but Jack had spent the night concealed and awake. He looked at his watch, almost 4am.

'Bogdan.'

The big Russian jumped. 'Yeah, boss?'

'I think we've lost him.'

'What is time?'

'Four o'clock. Sun's coming up.'

'What now?'

'Let's get back to the car.'

'Okay, da. We take the guns, boss?

Jack grinned. 'We take the guns, buddy.'

In the garden, Jack helped the big man over the wall and they trotted back to the Range Rover.

'Now what?' said Bogdan.

'We'll wait a couple more hours, see if he shows.'

Bogdan reclined the big comfy seat and smiled. 'Okay.'

It was five-thirty when Jack decided to call the Castelo San Lorenzo.

A sleepy voice answered. 'Si, prego?'

'Giovanni. Hi, it's Jack. Sorry to call so early.'

'Jack. Buongiorno. What can I do for you?'

'I know you've helped us a great deal. But could I ask if you've heard from your guys here in Monaco? We've been at Washington's villa all night and there's no sign.'

'Hmm . . . Hold on a moment. I'll need to speak to security.'

Several minutes past, and then. 'Jack?'

'Yes, I'm here.'

'There seems to be an issue. Our men have not checked-in as usual.'

'When did you hear from them last?'

'We have a strict protocol. All our field operatives must send a pre-formatted message every eight hours.'

'And you've not heard from your men since?'

'Midday yesterday.'

'Seventeen hours!'

'Yes.'

'Do you have a redundancy protocol? If they fail to check-in, is there a fall-back position?'

'No, Jack. They must make contact every eight hours. No redundancy.'

Jack paused a few moments and then said, 'So, your understanding would be they're dead?'

'I'm afraid so.'

'I'm sorry, Giovanni. So, what's your next move?'

'Security tells me we have the location of their vehicle.'

'Of, course . . . you'll have a tracker.'

'That's correct. I'm told the car is a few kilometres north of the city.'

'Send me the co-ordinates. We can check it out for you?'

'Thank you, Jack, but we don't usually seek outside assistance.'

'Giovanni. You've helped us. The least we can do is find the car. It might help to find your agents.'

'Wait a moment, please.'

'Okay.'

'What happens, boss?' said Bogdan.

Jack put the phone to his chest and said, 'Sounds like the Templari's agents have been killed.'

'Fuck,' said the Russian.

Jack put the phone back to his ear. 'Giovanni?' No reply.

A few more minutes passed, and then. 'Jack, hello?'

'Yes, I'm here.'

'I've spoken with the Contessa. Our security will send the vehicle's location to your phone. She says you must not interact with the local police. We will take care of that.'

'Not a problem. Last thing we want is to get tangled up with the cops.'

'Sorry, Jack. I didn't get that?'

'I said, yes. No police interaction.'

'There is at least a little good news.'

'Yeah? And that is?'

'We have a tracker in Washington's vehicle as well.'

Jack smiled. 'Great. That's great, Giovani. Okay, we'll check out your guys' car first. Then, is there any way you can relay Washington's position to us?'

'Just a second, please.'

Again, Jack waited, and again Bogdan asked, 'What happens now?'

Jack raised his hand. 'Hold on, buddy.'

'Jack?'

'Yeah, go ahead, Giovanni.'

'Our security will send location updates to your cell-phone.'

'Okay good. We'll be in touch. And thank you again, Giovanni.'

'Jack?'

'Yes?'

'The Contessa asked me to tell you, to be careful.'

Jack smiled. 'Tell her, always.'

The line went silent.

It only took about fifteen minutes to get to the location they'd been given. On the way, Jack had messaged Mathew with an update and their intentions. The road through the woods was quiet, but there was the odd car. Mostly locals by the look of the vehicles, as not too many of the wealthier Monaco residents would venture to this part of the Principality.

They pulled into the side of the road and got out. Jack was concentrating on the phone's screen, when Bogdan said, 'Here, boss. Look.'

Tyre tracks ran from the road into the woods. The soil had been churned-up and there were lots of broken plants. Several trees had obviously been hit by a car.

'This way, boss.'

It didn't take them long to find the VW.

Bogdan was about to open it when, Jack said, 'Hold on, big man. Don't touch it.'

They looked in the windows. A pair of binoculars on the back seat. Some discarded food wrappers and several bottles of water. Jack's phone pinged constantly, confirming they were at the location.

'Da. So this is it. What now?'

'They'll be here somewhere. He wouldn't want to hang around, so they won't be too far into the trees.

151

Okay, we'll search parallel with the road, Ten yards apart.'

It was Bogdan who found the bodies. 'Boss!'

Together they looked down at the two young men. Probably no more than thirty-five or six. Shot in the back, and the head. Execution style.

Jack knelt beside them, and said quietly, 'Bastard.'

The big Russian made the sign of the cross on his torso. 'A least it is quick, boss.'

Jack stood and said nothing for several seconds. Then took a photo of the scene. He saved the co-ordinates on his phone and stood for a few more seconds.

'Okay, buddy let's go get this fucker.'

Back in the Range Rover, Jack tapped out a message and sent the photo and location of the bodies to Giovanni. Then he sent the same to Mathew.

'Where to, boss?'

Jack looked at the phone again. 'West.'

Chapter Thirty Seven
'Marseilles'

After Paris, Marseilles is the second biggest city in France. The Greeks, and Romans, used the ancient port as a centre for trade, and military expansion to North Africa, when France was known as Gaul. Nowadays it is one of the busiest container ports in the world, with cargo ships and ferries going to all parts of the Mediterranean.

Rick Washington had been here many times. He liked Marseille. There was something about this cosmopolitan, rougher-than-Paris, get-down-n-dirty city, that appealed to him. For millennia it had been a crossroads on the Med that brought the good, the bad, and the ugly, together. Washington loved that. Beirut used to be the same. So too, Istanbul. But those places were becoming respectable.

Even though Marseille had been the European City of Culture the previous year, she was still the beautiful hooker, who'd kiss you tenderly, then knee you in the balls, as she lifted your wallet.

He'd arrived late evening and checked in to the Hotel Vendome, in the upmarket Castellane district of the city. He'd eaten a late supper in the hotel's excellent restaurant and then spent an hour or so in the trendy nightclub across the square. The girl, a cute Eurasian, had left his room a little after five.

It was now a few minutes before 10am and the elegant patio was busy with tourists and business people taking breakfast. As he drank the strong black coffee, his thoughts turned to the Templari. He was still pissed-off at their rejection, but last night's vigorous encounter had gone a long way to soothing his anger and frustration.

He still needed to be careful, hence the reason he'd not flown out of Nice. There were better ways to leave France when one needed to be inconspicuous, and the ferry to Algiers was one of them.

In the square, six storeys below the patio restaurant, Jack and Bogdan were enjoying their breakfast in the Bistro Helene.

Bogdan had checked the underground parking and found Washington's Audi. The pretty Russian receptionist had been more than helpful and, after Bogdan slipped her two hundred euros, confirmed Washington was indeed in residence. The bistro looked right across the square to the garage entrance, so they'd be able to see if the American left. Now they waited and quietly discussed how best to take him and get him out of France.

Jack took out his smartphone and rang Mathew.

'Jack. You okay?'

The hustle and bustle of the square made it difficult to hear, so Jack moved to a delivery alleyway at the side of the bistro.

'Matt?'

'Yes, I can hear you, Jack.'

'Okay, that's better,'

'So where are you?'

154

'Marseille. We're across from the Vendome, in the Castellane district. We have eyes on his car and know he's in the hotel.'

'Excellent work, Jack. Excellent work. If you can get him to the British Consul, we'll extract him from there.'

'Right. We need to be careful though, he's a slippery bastard. Don't want to do anything that'll get the local police involved. We'd never get him back.'

'That he is. But you're right, we don't want any local plod involved.'

Jack smiled at his brother's uncharacteristic turn of phrase. 'Okay, I'll be in touch.'

'Cheers, Jack, Be safe.'

'Always.'

The line went silent.

In Vendome's patio restaurant the diners were all but gone, Washington however ordered another pot of black coffee and tapped away at the screen of his smartphone. He brought up the ferry timetables and found there were four sailings a week. He smiled when he saw the next departure to Algiers was 6pm that evening.

Chapter Thirty Eight
'Houdini'

The voyage across the Mediterranean would take the best part of twenty-four hours, so Washington booked a small stateroom. His ticket was available on his phone and all he needed to do now was wait, then check in for embarkation two hours before sailing.

Across the square in the Bistro Helene, Jack was beginning to feel a little conspicuous. They had been there for almost four hours. They'd eaten breakfast, drunk several pots of tea and now lunch was being served.

'Let's order a sandwich or something.'

'Okay, boss. But we can't sit here all day.'

'No, but this is the best place to watch the garage and the front entrance.'

'Why not just go in and get this fucker, boss?'

'We could. I've done it before, but I had a couple of CIA guys waiting to cart the bastard off.'

Bogdan, with a surprised tone to his voice, said, 'You had him before?'

Jack nodded and smiled. 'Yeah. We were on a job in Syria. A joint effort between MI6 and the Yanks. This guy was running the CIA end of the operation.'

Bogdan leaned forward, as Jack lowered his voice.

'The Yanks were to extract us, but this guy,' Jack nodded towards the hotel, 'called off the chopper. Left us to fight our way out with an ISIS hit squad on our arses.'

'Fuck, boss. What happens?'

'They discovered he'd been working with ISIS. On their payroll for a couple of years. Giving them all kinds of shit. Helping them. For money of course. He disappeared. But Tom Hillman and I tracked him down to a hotel in Istanbul.'

'And you don't kill him?'

Jack smiled and looked around at the other customers. No one was paying them any attention. 'Obviously not, big man. We did put the fear-of-Christ up him though. Then handed him over to the CIA.'

'So how is he still free?'

'They had him in a black-site, in Panama, were flying him back to the States when the chopper went down. He survived and escaped.'

'Lucky bastard.'

'He's that alright. He was off-the-radar for over a year, then turned up again. He was targeting MI6 and CIA operatives and assets all over the world.'

Bogdan nodded. 'Revenge, da?'

'Yeah. But then the North Koreans recruited him.'

'Jeezus, boss. This guy is mercenary superstar.'

Jack laughed at the comment as the waitress arrived. 'You want something else, gentlemen?'

Jack nodded. 'Bring us two steak sandwiches. A coke and a beer, please.'

As she left, Bogdan said, 'So, what happens with Koreans?'

'Washington . . . Greg Stoneham, as he was called then . . . did some nasty shit to the water supply in the UK and America.'

'Ah, okay. Da, I see this on TV. Bad shit. Many people think it is Russia who does this.'

The waitress returned with the drinks, smiled and left.

'I tracked him to Saudi. Almost had him, but I got pretty badly injured. Was out of it for weeks.'

The big man swallowed half the beer, then said, 'He gets away again?'

Jack nodded. 'Yeah, he escaped, but we tracked him down to Istanbul again.'

'He likes Istanbul. Da?'

'I guess so. We caught him in the Blue Mosque. But not before he killed one of our team.'

'Shit!'

'Yeah, a good guy too. Anyway, the police take him, but he kills the two cops and escapes again.'

'Fuck, boss. This guy is a Houdini?'

'Not Houdini. Maybe just has nine lives?'

Bogdan grinned. 'Da, nines lives like cat. But in Russian we have saying. Cat has nine lives, but wolf has big teeth.'

'Not heard that one before, buddy.'

The big man grinned. 'Da, okay. Maybe I just make it up now.'

Jack laughed. 'But he's not gonna get away this time. This time he stays caught.'

'Or dead, boss.'

Chapter Thirty Nine
'No Cabins Left'

It was almost three o'clock when Rick Washington walked down the steps of the Hotel Vendome.

'Boss. Look, is him.'

'Go get the car, big man.'

Jack watched as the man across the square casually left the hotel and made his way to the garage entrance. Jack couldn't believe his eyes. There was nothing left of the old Greg Stoneham. *That's an amazing transformation. I'll give ya that,* he said to himself.

A minute or two later the Range Rover pulled up to the side of the Bistro Helene. Jack dropped a handful of euros on the table and joined Bogdan. As he climbed in, the Audi emerged from the garage.

'Not too close, buddy. Let's see what he's up to. If we can take him quietly, we will.'

The Russian nodded. 'Da. Play it by my ear, boss.'

Jack grinned. 'Yeah, buddy. Play it by your ear.'

They followed the sleek Audi out of the square and into the busier streets of the Castellane district. It wasn't long before they saw the signs for the Marseille docks area. The town streets were busy but, once they got onto the main highway, the trucks and wagons increased dramatically. About thirty-five minutes after leaving the Vendome, the Audi turned off the main highway and onto the Quai de Maroc. Jack watched as the Audi, now half a dozen cars in front of them, moved slowly along the quay side and into the huge carpark.

'Pull-in where you can, buddy. Not too close.'

Bogdan took the ticket from the machine and the barrier swung up. Jack lost sight of the low-slung Audi for a few seconds then, as Bogdan pulled into a vacant space, saw Washington getting out of his car. For a split second he thought their eyes made contact but, when he looked back, there was no panic in how Washington made his way from the carpark.

It was the hottest part of the day, but the cool wind coming off the sea, gave some welcome relief from the sun's rays. They continued to follow the American along the Quai de Maroc towards several waiting ships.

'Looks like he's heading for the ferry, boss.'

'Yeah, but which one?'

The crowds of passengers making their way to the Terminal made it easy to follow Washington. They watched as he entered Departures. 'That's it,' said Jack, 'he's definitely taking one of the ferries.'

'Gun,' said Bogdan, quietly.

'What?'

'Gimme your weapon. There will be security here.'

Jack nodded and discreetly passed his gun to the Russian. 'Wait here, boss. I take to truck.'

As the big man trotted off, Jack took out his smartphone and tapped the screen.

'Mathew?'

'Jack, hi there, You okay?'

'Yeah, we're good, Matt. Need some help. Fast.'

'Tell me?'

'What is the next ferry due to leave Marseille. Where is it going. And I need two tickets on it.'

'Hold on,' said Mathew, then shouted, 'Victoria!'

160

Jack wiped the sweat from his face, then turned to see Bogdan trotting up behind. 'Okay, boss. What is plan?'

'Hold on, buddy. Go ahead, Matt.'

Jack. Next departure is eighteen-hundred, local-time, today. Heading for Algiers. No cabins left. She got you two reclining seats in the Business Lounge. Tickets will be with you in a couple of minutes.'

'That's great. Thanks, Matt. I'll be in touch when we're underway.'

'Be safe Jack . . . I hope the crossings not too bad. I know you get sea-sick.'

'Thanks for reminding me.'

The line went silent.

'Boss?'

'We're sailing to Algiers, big man.'

'Niet, niet, niet,' said Bogdan, 'I have the seasick.'

Jack laughed. 'I have the seasick too, buddy.'

Chapter Forty
'Our Old Friend'

The ferry, *MV Salena,* departed Marseilles pretty much on time, a few minutes after 6pm. The ship was busy, and Victoria had done a great job getting tickets. There were people everywhere, so Jack and Bogdan quickly headed for the Business Class bar and settled down until the ship had cleared the harbour.

'What's the plan now, boss?'

'We wait until we're out at sea. Then we go find him. We know he's not gonna be tooled-up, so it should be easy enough for the two of us to take him. Then we sit on him until we dock. Mathew will contact the British Embassy, and they'll have an arrest warrant ready when we disembark.'

'That's it? We just hand him over? We don't get to fuck him up?'

Jack shook his head and grinned. 'You can give him a slap. But our job is to catch the bastard, big man.'

'And then what?'

'We go home, buddy.'

'So, the Brits will get ransom back?'

'Pretty much yeah. I guess they'll have to pay something to the banks, but yeah they'll get the money back.'

Jack said nothing more, as his old friend slumped down in the recliner, a look of disappointment, on his usually happy face. He waited a couple of minutes and then said. 'There will, I'm sure, be a substantial reward though.'

The Russian turned to Jack. 'Substantial?'

'Yeah. Maybe two or three million pounds.'

The smile returned to the big man's face. 'Da, this is good. But I think it should be three mill, not two, boss.'

Jacked smiled and nodded. 'Da, Bogdan. Three, not two.'

The Business Lounge was busy but, with the absence of kids, not too raucous. After finding and confirming their seats, they headed to the restaurant. They took a table in the corner and kept their eyes peeled, just in case Washington showed up. Bogdan had a couple of beers, Jack drank coke, as usual. Two large steaks, a nice Béarnaise sauce, champignons and fries, gave them the first decent meal for three days.

Back in the lounge they relaxed and waited until the passengers had gone to their cabins or settled down for the night. Neither of them had slept properly for over forty-eight hours and, at almost one in the morning, Jack was surprised to find they'd been asleep for almost four hours. The lights in the lounge had been dimmed and the place was quiet, with only the odd one or two people reading under the tiny courtesy-lights.

Jack shook the Russian, and said quietly, 'Bogdan.'

As usual the big man woke with a start, 'Hrrrm!'

'Shhh . . . It's okay.'

'Time is it, boss?'

'It's after one. Come on, let's go.'

They made their way from the public decks, down towards the central reception. As they passed through the bar, Jack bought a bottle of champagne, and asked for an ice-bucket and three flutes.

Behind the reception desk a young man was intent on studying his computer screen.   Jack placed the champagne on the counter, smiled, and said, 'Excuse me.'

'Oui, monsieur?'

'We've just had a message that one of our old friends is travelling on this ferry as well,' he tapped the bottle, 'and we'd like to surprise him. Would you be able to tell us where we can find him please?'

The receptionist looked at the wine, then Jack, and then the big man standing behind him. 'I'm sorry, monsieur, but we don't usually give out that kind of information.'

'Of course, of course. I understand. But we've not seen him for many years and it would be such a great reunion for us.' Jack rattled the bottle in the ice.

'But, monsieur I . . .'

Still smiling, Jack slid two, one-hundred euro notes discreetly across the counter.

The man quickly placed a sheet of paper on the notes, and said quietly, 'Very well, monsieur. What is your friend's name?'

'Washington. Mr Rick Washington.'

'Un moment, monsieur.'

Jack turned to Bogdan and winked.

A few seconds later, the young man looked up and said, 'I'm sorry monsieur, Mr Washington is not on-board.'

Jack continued to smile. 'But we have a message from his wife that he is definitely on-board. Could you please check again?'

'No, monsieur. I mean, oui. Monsieur Washington did board the ship but disembarked again before we sailed.'

'Are you sure?'

'Of course,' the man tapped the screen, 'it is here on the manifest.'

Jack said nothing for several seconds, then turned to Bogdan. 'He did see me in the carpark . . . Shit.'

As they walked away from the desk, the receptionist, called, 'Monsieur. Your champagne?'

Jack looked over his shoulder, and said, 'You have it.'

* * *

About seven hours earlier, Rick Washington had indeed seen Jack Castle in the terminal carpark. Startled for a second, and then calmly carrying on, the American had boarded the *Salena* as if all was well. Once on-board he'd concealed himself on the boat-deck and watched Castle and the big man come aboard.

It was only at the last minute, as the gangway was about to be hauled away, he made his move and stepped onto it. An officer rushed forward and stopped him. 'We are about to sail, monsieur,' he said.

Washington told the officer he must get off. 'It's an emergency. I'm not travelling. I must get off immediately.'

'But wait, monsieur, I need your boarding-card please?'

The American handed over the ticket, and then quickly trotted down the gangway. At the bottom he'd turned and scanned the smiling faces of the passengers along the ship's rail. No sign of the Englishman, or his big companion.

Another officer had spoken to Rick in the terminal. 'Is everything all right, monsieur?'

'Yes. Yes. I had to get off. There's an emergency at home. Excuse me.' And with that, he'd quickly left the Departures Hall.

Outside, he'd concealed himself in the shadow of the building and waited until the *Salena* had cleared the dock-side. He'd watched as it gently edged-away from the quay, and then gather speed, as it sailed gracefully through the mouth of the harbour, and out into the Mediterranean.

* * *

Out on deck, Jack and Bogdan clung onto the hand-rail as they looked out over the dark Mediterranean. The moon was hidden behind heavy cloud and the cold night wind had risen. The sea-swell had increased considerably, and the big ship rolled and bounced against the oncoming waves. Both men felt extremely unwell, their moods reflected in the dismal night.

'Oh, this is shit,' said Jack, as he sucked in the chill air.

'Ugghhh . . . answered the big Russian, as he sent the undigested remains of his steak dinner over the side.

The next few hours were spent wrapped in blankets, on the leeward side of the ship, trying to hold on to as much of their stomach linings as possible.

As the sun came up, the wind dropped, and the clouds cleared. The ship steadied itself and the sickening movement they'd endured for most of the night subsided. By 7am the sea-state had calmed, and the sun began to warm the morning, returning the Mediterranean to its usual benign state.

Jack and Bogdan climbed out of their cocoon of blankets and headed to the bow of the ship. As the *Salena* ploughed south towards the African coast they began, for the first time in six hours, to feel human again.

There were another ten hours until they docked in Algiers and Mathew still had to be told Washington had given them the slip. Not a call Jack was looking forward to making.

'How you feelin, buddy?'

'Better, boss, but this is last time I go on fuckin ship.'

Jack gave a weak smile and the big Russian reciprocated. 'Let's get inside and see if we can get warmed up. Maybe a cuppa tea eh?'

'No breakfast for me, boss.'

'Lost your appetite big man?'

'Da. I eat nothing until I get back to Moscow.'

Jack laughed this time. 'Yeah right. Like that's gonna last.'

Inside, the passengers were stirring from their seats. The restaurant was filling up with diners and the bar already had a crowd waiting for drinks.

Bogdan looked around, then shook his head. 'How can these people eat after last night?'

Jack grinned and said quietly. 'They're French.'

They both laughed.

Chapter Forty One
'Ça Va, Monsieur?'

Washington watched for several minutes as the *Salena* cleared the harbour and began its voyage south. His mind was racing as he analysed the reasons, the possibilities of why that Limey bastard, Jack Castle was here. He walked slowly back to the carpark, his shadow getting longer, as the crimson fire-ball of sun sank in the West

Yes, the Templari were watching him, but he'd dealt with those two jokers. So why Castle? Did the British know about him? How could they? Were the Templari working with the Brits? No, they didn't do that . . .or did they? 'Fuck, fuck, fuck,' he said out loud.

By the time he got back to the Audi, the flood-lights, in the huge carpark, had come on. He looked around and then saw the big Range Rover two rows away. *The 4x4 in the road. They were there in his villa.* 'Shit,' he said out loud.

He pressed the key-fob and his car's lights flashed. As he opened the door he stopped and smiled. 'Those sneaky fuckers tagged the car!'

He closed the door, took out his smartphone and switched on the torch. Again, he looked around. The odd car arrived and departed, but no threats evident. He dropped to his knees then lay down on the warm concrete. Taking care to cover every inch of the underside, he painstakingly scanned the vehicle's chassis, wheel arches, suspension and steering. Nothing.

He stood up and brushed the dust from his clothes, flicked open the boot and continued the search, nothing in the boot, or spare wheel cavity. He opened the door and reached in to flip the bonnet. The massive engine made him smile for a second.

As he leaned in, a voice said, 'Ça va, monsieur?'

He turned with a start, to see a security officer standing behind him. 'Oh. Yes, I'm okay.

'American?'

'Yes, American.'

'This is your automobile?'

'Yes, it's mine.'

'You have problem? You need help, monsieur?'

'No. No, it's fine. Thank you. Just checking before I leave. I've a long drive.'

'Bon. This is wise. Okay, bonsoir, monsieur.'

Washington smiled. 'Bonsoir,' then continued his search of the engine-bay.

After ten more minutes of searching he'd still found nothing. The inquisitive security guard was now standing by the exit, watching him. 'Fuck,' he said under his breath.

He closed the hood and climbed in. The big engine gurgled into life and slowly he pulled away from his parking space. At the barrier he put in the ticket, then realised he hadn't paid.

The guard came over. 'Problem, monsieur?'

Washington climbed out. 'Forgot to pay,' then went over to the machine.

He quickly inserted the ticket.

170

The guard walked around the Audi, bent down and looked inside.

'Shit,' said Washington quietly, then fed a ten-euro note into the slot.

A few seconds later his ticket popped out. He got back in the car and tried the ticket again. The barrier swung silently upwards. As he drove past the guard he smiled and raised his hand. The expression on the guard's face was anything but friendly.

The sleek Audi pulled onto the Quai de Maroc and Washington put his foot down. As the big engine growled, his thoughts returned to Castle, the Templari, and his next move.

Chapter Forty Two
'Jackals & Rats'

Jack phoned London a little after 9am The conversation with Mathew had gone far better than he'd expected.

'Don't beat yourself up, big brother,' said Mathew. 'You did a great job tracing the ransom. The government is recovering the money as we speak. They'll get it all back, less of course several millions in commission. But that's peanuts to what was paid.'

'Yes, but we still let Washington slip.'

'We'll get him, Jack. We know what he looks like now. So does the CIA. His face is plastered all over Europe, and Interpol now have him as, Most Wanted.'

'Not forgetting the Templari,' said Jack, 'I doubt they'll let the killing of their agents go un-punished?'

'That's right. The world that was so open to him has shrunk, bro.'

'Yeah, I guess.'

'You going to head home from Algiers, Jack?'

'Might as well. Unless something comes up and we can go after him again?'

'You dock at seventeen-hundred, local time?'

'That's right.'

'Okay, I'll have someone from the Embassy pick you up. They'll sort you out a decent flight home. What about Bogdan? He's going to Moscow?'

'No, he'll be comin' to London too. I said there'd be a substantial reward.'

'Okay, good. I'm sure Her Majesty's Government will be more than generous.'

'Three-mill generous?'

'I don't see why not. All things considered.'

'Good. Thanks' Matt.'

'How you feeling by the way? How's the voyage?'

'Don't ask, bro.'

* * *

After leaving the docks area, Washington had gone back into the city and parked-up in one of the less salubrious neighbourhoods.

He got out and had only walked for about a hundred yards, when he saw the two youths appear. He stepped back into a derelict shop doorway, as a large rat ran over his foot. He watched as the kids walked around the sleek car. Jackals, eyeing up a ripe carcass. He grinned.

The keys, dangling in the ignition, made it easier than normal for them to drive off.

As the engine's growl faded into the distance, he smiled and walked quickly away from the dog-shit laden street. The big rat re-appeared for a second, sniffed the air, then ran across the pavement and into a drain.

Back in the Castellane district, he checked into a small boutique hotel to consider his options. He had a few thousand in euros, plus over fifty thousand dollars available on valid credit cards. But that wouldn't be enough to get him out of Europe undetected. If the fuckin Brits were onto him, then they'd discovered his new identity. More worryingly they now knew what he looked like. He needed to get onto one of the banks and get some real money transferred.

As he swiped the phone's screen he smiled. The thought of the money brightened his mood considerably, especially now he didn't have to hand over two-bill' to the Templari. *A new face in the Philippines again,* he thought. He scrolled down and found the number.

'Good afternoon. Thank you for calling Macau Merchant. How may I help you?'

'Hello. My name is Boston. May I speak with the Managing Director please?'

'Certainly, sir. Please hold the line a moment.'

A few seconds passed and then. 'Mr Boston, good afternoon. How may I help you, sir?'

'I'd like to transfer some funds please.'

'Certainly sir. We just need to go through some security?'

'Yes, of course.'

'May I have your account designation, sir?'

'Blue, 1. 1. 5. 1. 6. 1. Gold.'

The line was silent for some time and then. 'Ah. I'm sorry, Mr Boston, sir. That account is now closed.'

'I'm sorry?'

'Closed and the funds transferred, sir.'

Washington's throat was constricted. He couldn't speak for several seconds. He swallowed hard. 'What? That's impossible. What the hell have you done with my money?'

'I can't really say, sir. There has been an intervention from our government.'

'Intervention? Your government? What do you mean? There should be almost a billion sterling in there.'

'Not any more, Mr Boston. I'm sorry. I don't know what to tell you, sir. I have no idea what . . .'

'I'm coming there to sort this shit out. You're a bunch of thieving cock-suckers.'

'Mr Bost . . .'

Washington threw the phone across the room. He collapsed onto the couch as his legs buckled under him. His breath came hard and fast. Heart pounded. He looked at the phone up against the wall, then jumped up and retrieved it. Frantically scrolling through the contacts, he called the other two banks.

After the calls, he remained slumped on the couch. For almost fifteen minutes he sat in a daze. Then his heart rate returned to normal and his breathing steadied. He stood up and went to the window. The busy street below, with the smiling happy people going about their business, suddenly annoyed him. He opened the window and sucked in the warm air. His mind was calm now. The realization of what had happened to his money hit him hard. Gone. His money was all gone. 'Those fuckin Brits,' he said out loud.

The journey from Monaco to Marseille had taken a little over two hours in the Audi. The bus would take almost five, calling at Toulon, and several other lesser towns on the way east. The express would have been faster, but the one that trundled along the old coast road was more discreet.

It was not his ideal mode of travel, but it did however offer the most low-key, with no security checks at the Bus Station. *Get back to the villa* he'd thought. *The*

175

four-hundred-grand in the floor safe. Risky, but necessary. It'll get me out of France. Out of Europe. Then I'll deal with Mr Jack Castle and the Templari.

Chapter Forty Three
'Cheers, Rick'

The bus pulled into the Principality Central Coach Station a little after 8pm Before disembarking Washington carefully scanned the area. The place was busy, but that was to be expected. He waited until everyone had left, and the driver shouted, 'Ici Monaco, monsieur.'

He raised his hand and said, 'Merci.' At the coach door he looked around one more time, then quickly disappeared into the hustle and bustle of the station.

The taxi let him out a good two hundred yards from his villa. He waited until the cab had turned around and left, then scanned the area. A set of approaching headlights made him step back off the road and into the shadow of a gnarled old olive tree. He waited for several minutes and then walked slowly towards the house. Fifty yards away, he moved down the hillside and approached the property from the rear.

He waited for at least half-an-hour, watching the back of the villa, looking for movement, shadows, anything. Slowly he entered the pool area. He could see all the way through to the front of the house and the illuminated drive and gardens. Again, he waited. Nothing.

He tried the patio doors. Locked. Then he slowly moved round the side of the building to the front corner, always vigilant, ever cautious. Again, nothing. He quickly let himself in and flipped the switch on the exterior light's timer. The front of the house fell into darkness.

The moon gave enough light to see, and he quickly checked all the weapons-stashes. Three guns had gone, whoever had found the guns were good. Professionals. He smiled when he discovered the Glock in the bottom of the dishwasher was still there. He deftly racked the mechanism and checked it was still fully loaded.

In the bathroom, he knelt and carefully eased the side-panel from the bath. He took his smartphone, switched on the torch and leaned into the cavity. The light glinted on the steel of the floor-safe. He quickly tapped in the combination and the door sprung open with a metallic click. He removed a small Smith & Wesson revolver, then the bundles of cash.

Back in the bedroom he found a money belt and loaded most of the cash into it. The rest he stuffed into the bottom of a lightweight rucksack, along with a few clothes, the Glock and the revolver. From the back of his underwear drawer, he took an ivory handled switch-blade and slipped that into his back pocket.

In the lounge he went to the patio, looked out and down to the glittering harbour, three miles below. For several seconds he enjoyed the view, then turned back to the small bar and poured himself a large shot of Bourbon. He raised the glass and said, 'Cheers, Rick,' then swallowed the fiery amber liquid.

He went to the big windows again, swiped his phone's screen and scrolled through the contacts. It took several beeps before the answer came. 'Yes?'

'It's me,' said Washington.

'I know it's you. Why are you calling me?'

'You know why. What the hell happened?'

'I said I'd do what I could. I'm only one of thirteen.'

'You're a lying sack-of-shit.'

There was silence for several seconds, then Washington said, 'You still there?'

'I'm here, but I won't be if you keep talking like that.'

Washington chuckled. 'Oh, spare me the indignation.'

'What do you want? There's nothing further I can do for you, Rick.'

'Firstly, I want the two million I gave you. You didn't deliver. You don't get to keep my money.'

'I'll see what I can do.'

'Bullshit. You'll pay me back or . . .'

The other voice snapped. 'Or what, Rick? What will you do. You can do nothing.'

'I can let your friends on the council know what you've really been up too.'

Again, several seconds past. 'And what was the other, Rick?'

'What?'

'You said, firstly. What was the other thing?'

'Ah, yes. I want Jack Castle's location in the UK. His home.'

Chapter Forty Four
'Welcome To Algiers'

The *MV Salena* slowly eased up to the dock in the Port of Algiers. It took several minutes for the lines to be secured and the covered gangway attached. Jack and Bogdan, feeling decidedly better than the night before, had managed to get a shower and clean up. They now stood with the hundreds of other eager passengers, waiting to disembark. From their boat-deck vantage point, Jack could see the British Embassy vehicle, a shiny new Land Rover, waiting next to the Terminal. As each passenger disembarked, four stewards scanned their boarding cards, electronically removing them from the ships manifest. The procedure took a lot longer than Jack would have liked, but twenty minutes later they were in the Arrivals Hall.

A young man, dressed in an immaculate pale grey linen suit, approached. 'Mr Castle, Mr Markov?'

As he offered his hand, Jack said, 'Yes, I'm Castle.'

'Good evening, gentlemen. I'm Tony Havers, British Embassy. Welcome to Algiers.' The accent was North of England.

'Thank you, Tony,' said Jack. 'Where you from?'

The Embassy man smiled. 'Cumbria, a little place near Kendal.'

Jack returned the smile. 'I was brought up in Windermere.'

'Yes, I know, and Mr Sterling sends his regards, sir.'

Jack nodded slightly. 'Ah, you're with his team.'

'That's correct, sir. If you'll follow me, please. We don't need to go through this,' he gestured towards the crowd waiting for Immigration.

As they bypassed the Immigration desks, Havers shook hands with a smartly dressed Immigration Officer, and said in perfect Arabic, 'Shukran, sidi.'

The officer nodded. 'Afwan, habibi.'

As they drove from the Terminal, the Embassy man turned to Jack, and said, 'The Ambassador is attending a Government function this evening, sir. He sends his best regards and apologies for not meeting you.'

'Please convey our thanks, when you see him next.'

'Of course, sir.'

'So, when do we fly out, Tony?'

'You're booked on Air France, this evening. Wheels up at twenty-three hundred.'

The ride through the busy streets was surprisingly swift. The driver, expertly weaving in and out of the cars, trucks and donkey carts, had them pulling up to the Embassy gates twenty minutes after leaving the Terminal.

'We have some time before we depart for the airport, gentlemen. Dinner will be ready at twenty-hundred hours,' said Havers.

'I think we may skip that if you don't mind, Tony.'

Havers smiled. 'Ah, okay, sir. As you wish. The crossing is sometimes a challenge and tends to leave one without an appetite.

'Da,' said Bogdan, 'no appetite for me until Moscow.'

181

* * *

Washington's taxi arrived at the gates of his villa just after 9pm. The driver was surprised, when his passenger asked to be taken to the highway, north of the city. Thirty minutes later, at the first services-area on the A8 autoroute, Rick Washington watched as the cab drove off.

He knew there'd be strong security at the airport and rail station. Going by coach was not an option either. A rental car or taxi would still leave a footprint, someone would remember him. too. That only left bumming a ride on a long distance truck.

There were dozens of wagons parked and, although he knew there'd be many drivers settling down for the night, there would also be others who would be moving on. For almost half an hour he walked around the huge parking area, knocking on cab doors and talking to drivers of all nationalities. He was considering changing his plans, when at last he found a Polish driver who was heading north.

'Sure, mister. I can take you to Lyon. For a hundred euro.'

Washington smiled. 'You gotta a deal.'

Chapter Forty Five
'Can't Have Been Kosher'

At 3am Air France flight AF33 touched down at Heathrow. Both Jack and Bogdan had slept pretty much the whole way back. Neither had eaten anything, but Jack drank a couple of cokes and Bogdan his usual beer.

The London leg from Paris was quiet and the transition through Heathrow Immigration swift for once. As they came out of Arrivals, Jack looked for Mathew. A few seconds later he saw his brother standing a little way to the side of the main exit. 'This way, big man,' said Jack.

The two brothers hugged, and Mathew said, 'Good to have you back.'

'Matt, this is my great friend, Bogdan Markov. Bogdan, this is Mathew Sterling.'

The big Russian smiled, as he vigorously shook Mathew's hand. 'Is a pleasure to meet you, Mathew. I have heard much of you.'

'And I you, Bogdan. And I you.'

'Okay,' said Jack. 'Am I getting home tonight? I mean this morning?'

'Of course. I'd have Nicole after me if I didn't get you home as soon as possible. I thought I'd come out and stay at your place, Jack. If that's okay? We can debrief in the morning.'

'Sure, no problem.'

'And I have a meeting with the Director General for lunch tomorrow. I'd like you guys to join me?'

'Sounds good, Matt. But let's get home, eh?'

Mathew smiled. 'My driver is right outside.'

As the big Jaguar pulled away from the Arrivals Terminal, Mathew turned to Jack, and said, 'We had some news a little while ago, from our friends in Florence.'

'Yeah?' said Jack.

'Washington's vehicle was tracked.'

'Really? They know where he is?'

'Afraid not. The car was in an accident, on the motorway north of Monaco. Crashed into a bridge. Two bodies in it.'

'Washington's?'

'No. Two youths apparently. Sounds like a couple of joy-riders.'

'Not much joy for them, then.'

'Yeah, just kids.'

'So, Washington is on the move, but we don't know where?'

'For now, no we don't. But there's more.'

'Yeah?'

'We received a signal from Interpol, about a certain Mr Myles DeVere.'

'Oh, that joker. What's he been up to?'

'We don't have that information yet. But whatever it was, it can't have been Kosher.'

Jack frowned. 'Okay. So, what was the news?'

DeVere's naked body was fished-out of the River Arno, on the outskirts of Florence, a little after midnight.

'Poor bastard,' said Jack.

The big Russian shrugged. 'He was a bit of asshole though, boss.'

Jack shook his head at the big man's comment. 'Naked! That's a bit weird isn't it?'

'There was an antique stiletto embedded in his chest. The handle had an ornate *TI* monogramed in gold.'

'All very cloak and dagger,' quipped Jack.

'That's not the strangest part. His forehead was branded with Roman numerals and his tongue had been cut out.'

'Jesus . . . A ritual killing?'

'Certainly looks like it.'

'So what the hell's he been up to?'

'Whatever it was, he's certainly pissed somebody off.'

Jack was silent for a while, then said, 'What numerals?'

'What?'

'You said, Roman numerals. What were they?'

Mathew swiped his smartphone screen, A few seconds later he said, 'MCCCVII.'

Jack nodded and smiled. '1307. The year the Knights Templars were rounded-up and killed.'

Chapter Forty Six
'Big Macs & Full English'

The big lorry made its way west, along the A8 autoroute. Washington relaxed into the comfy passenger seat next to the Polish driver and closed his eyes. They'd only been on the road for a little over twenty minutes, when the overhead signs flashed to indicate two lanes had been closed.

'Looks like accident ahead, mister.'

Washington sat up and rubbed his eyes. 'Bad?'

'Don't know. But it slows traffic a lot.'

It took almost thirty-five minutes for them to get to the accident site. As they approached the scene, a couple of police officers were supervising the removal of the wrecked vehicle. The third lane had been coned-off, and another two officers were waving the long line of trucks and cars through. As the Polish truck slowly edged past, Washington grinned when he saw the remains of his Audi being loaded onto the recovery truck.

It was after three in the morning when they pulled into the last services before the Lyon turn-off. Washington had managed to get a couple of hours of much needed sleep and after paying the driver his hundred euros, said, 'Thank you and safe journey.'

'Thanks, mister, but I'm nearly there. Ten minutes more to Lyon and then I sleep also.'

As he swung the heavy door closed, Washington said, 'Whatever!'

The Lyon services were not as busy as Monaco, but there were enough trucks to hope a ride north would be possible. Unfortunately, as it was the middle of the night, it looked like all the drivers had battened-down and were now sleeping. He saw the big illuminated **M** and headed for McDonalds.

After two Royales, a double portion of fries and a half litre of Coca Cola, he felt better. As he settled down in one of the comfier seats, he shook his head slightly and thought, *Royale? Really? Fuckin French, what the hell's wrong with calling it a Big Mac?*

By 6am the truckers were stirring, and the various eateries were beginning to fill up. He went and bought a large black coffee and started walking around the tables. It didn't take long to find a French driver who was heading to Paris.

The driver, who was clearly gay, seemed delighted to give the American a lift. 'Oui monsieur, après manger, we go.'

Washington nodded. 'Okay, thank you. I'll just get another coffee,' then, as he walked to the counter, said under his breath, 'Jesus!'

* * *

In Berkshire it was almost 5am when the Jaguar drove through the big gates of Jack's home. The sun had been up for over an hour, and so had Nicole.

187

'They're here, Nicole,' shouted Brian, their live-in security man.

Nicole was at the door as the Jag pulled up to the front of the house. Jack climbed out and took her in his arms. 'Hey,' he said after kissing her, 'why're you up so early?'

'Like I'm going to be asleep when you get home.' She turned to the group of men by the car. 'And guests. Most wives get gifts when their man comes home. I get guests.'

'Sorry, babe,' said Jack, unconvincingly.

She smiled and moved to hug Mathew, 'Hello, darling. Lovely to see you again.'

'You too, Nikki. Gorgeous as ever.'

'And this is Bogdan.' She hugged him, then kissed his cheek. 'Welcome to our home. I've heard so much about you.'

The big Russian, clearly smitten by her charm, lapsed straight into their native tongue. For several moments their exchange continued, speaking so fast it was difficult for Jack, or Mathew, to keep up. Finally, with a laugh, she linked her arm through Bogdan's, and said, 'Right. There's breakfast for everyone in the dining room,' then, turning to Mathew's driver, continued, 'you too, young man.'

As they all entered the large hallway, Mathew put his arm round his brother's shoulder and said, 'Looks like the big guy has fallen for your wife, Jack.'

The driver, bringing up the rear, said under his breath, 'Don't blame him.'

Chapter Forty Seven
'Pigale'

The journey from Lyon to Paris took a never ending, 6 hours. The gay driver, talked incessantly, in fractured Franglais, about absolutely nothing. Washington had thought the man may have tried to hit on him but it was clear, the only reason he wanted anyone along, was to listen to his continuous and vacuous chat. It was after midday when the still-chattering driver, dropped Washington near to one of Paris's outer Metro stations.

Rick Washington knew Paris well. He'd been stationed here for two years in the early part of his CIA career. Many of the shadow-world contacts he'd recruited recently, were once adversaries. Now they were assets, to be used as-and-when he needed them.

His plan was to enter the UK covertly, by one of two ways. Use the 'illegals route' and join the hundreds of people waiting at Calais to jump a truck to Dover or, solicit the assistance of a less scrupulous boat owner and sail across the Channel.

Getting on a truck undetected was easy at the Port of Calais, but there was the chance he could be discovered on the UK side. A good option if there was no other. But, as he was carrying weapons, not to mention a shit-load of cash, a boat was the smart way to go.

He had no contacts on the coast and wandering around Calais asking to be taken to England on the Q/T was far too risky. He would stay in Paris tonight and find the support he needed to get across the water and do the job in Berkshire.

He took the Metro, from Melun station in the suburbs, north to Place Pigale in Montmartre. He hadn't showered or changed his clothes for almost 48 hours, so he checked in to a small hotel in the Rue Pomery, on the edge of Pigale's red light district. He paid in cash which, in any other respectable establishment, would have seemed a little suspicious, but here in Pigale cash was always king.

The room was small, but surprisingly clean, with fresh bedding and towels. There was a small safe, which he was sure was anything but, so he eased the big heavy wardrobe from the wall and hid almost all his money, and the Glock, in the back carcass. He put a couple of hundred euros in the safe, to satisfy any would-be thief.

After showering, he placed a chair against the door and balanced the small table light on the seat, a crude, but effective warning should anyone try to sneak in. With the Smith & Wesson in one hand and the switch-blade in the other, he lay down and quickly fell asleep.

Chapter Forty Eight
'Not In This House'

After breakfast, Mathew, Jack and Bogdan, went out to the patio and spent the next hour and a half going over the events of the last few days. Every detail was considered and scrutinized to ensure the meeting with the DG would be as smooth as possible and any questions would be answered in full.

Almost all the ransom money had been recovered, and that had been the primary goal of the Government. The apprehension, although certainly desired, of the perpetrators was secondary.

Maggie, their housekeeper, came out and said, 'Excuse me, Mr Jack,' and laid a tray with coffee and tea on the table. 'Miss Nicole said you would be needing this.'

'Yes, indeed. Thanks, Maggie.'

Mathew looked at his watch, almost 8am. 'We need to be heading into the city soon.'

As he poured himself some tea, Jack said, 'Okay. Let's have this, then Bogdan and I can get showered and changed.'

From the conservatory, Nicole saw the meeting was ending and went out to join them. 'So, what are you boys up to next?'

'Need to go into London, darling,' said Jack.

She feigned a stern look, placed one hand defiantly on her hip, and said, 'And when might you be home, Mr Castle?'

Jack stood up and put his arms around her. 'Definitely home today, boss.'

With a huge grin, Bogdan said, 'But you are the Boss, boss?'

Jack turned to the big man and laughed. 'Not in this house.'

The drive from East Monkton into London was reasonably quick, as Mathew had arranged for a police outrider to precede them, which was definitely an advantage once into the busy city streets. They arrived at the Vauxhall Cross building a little before 10:30. Lunch with the Director General was at noon. Matt, Bogdan and Jack took the lift to the executive floor. As they entered Mathew's outer office, his PA, Victoria, stood and said, 'Good morning, sir. Good morning, gentlemen.'

'Hello again, Victoria,' said Jack, 'how are you?'

'Fine, sir. Thank you.'

As he opened the inner office door, Mathew said, 'This is, Mr Bogdan Markov, Vic.'

'Dobroe utro, ser. Kak dela,' she said, in perfect Russian.

Bogdan smiled and returned the formal greeting.

She turned to her boss. 'May I bring you anything, sir?'

'Guys?' said Mathew.

Both shook their heads as they followed him inside.

'Okay, have a seat and relax. I need to finish this report and get it to Victoria. I want to give it to the DG at lunch.'

192

Jack nodded. 'No problem. Go ahead, Matt.'

As the two friends sat down, Bogdan said quietly 'I think not many Russians get to sit in the head of MI6 office. Eh, boss?'

They both grinned.

Lunch with the Director General had been pleasant enough. Mathew knew he would be somewhat put-off at having to eat with the big Russian. But he also knew the DG was well aware it was Bogdan and Jack who had saved several high ranking arses in the security service, by recovering the Poseidon ransom.

At the end of the meal, Mathew passed a leather folder across to his boss. 'The full report, to date, sir. As promised.'

'Thank you, Mathew. An excellent job,' then turning to Jack and Bogdan, 'and thank you both. The British Government owes you a great debt.'

They both smiled, as Mathew said. 'Yes, sir. Speaking of that. You'll see I've made a recommendation that there'd be a reward commensurate with the amount recovered,' he tapped the folder. 'Last page, sir.'

The Director put on his spectacles and opened the folder. He cleared his throat and said, 'I, of course, cannot confirm any such payment but once I speak with the Home Secretary, I'm sure there will be no issues. Now, if you'll excuse me gentlemen, I'm due in Whitehall in half an hour.'

They all stood, and handshakes were given. After he left, Jack said, sarcastically, 'What a lovely man.'

Mathew sat down again, smiled, and said, 'Isn't he just. And he's left his tab open. Care for a cognac, Mr Markov?'

Bogdan nodded gracefully. 'Da. Very large please, Mr Sterling.'

Chapter Forty Nine
'Madame Sofie'

Rick Washington woke suddenly to the sound of a car's backfire, 'Jesus,' he said out loud. He took a deep breath, 'Get a grip.'

He put the weapons on the side table and looked at his watch. He was surprised to see it was after 8 o'clock and already dark. He was even more surprised that he'd slept for almost seven hours. He went to the window and the street, so quiet earlier in the day, was beginning to liven-up. Further down the road several illuminated signs flashed, beckoning punters to the bars, strip-joints and massage parlours. *Paris, don't ya just love it,* he thought.

After getting dressed, he checked the wardrobe again, then picked up the revolver and slipped it carefully into the back of his waistband. He closed the blade of the knife, and dropped it into his back pocket. He looked at himself in the mirror, ran his fingers through his hair, and said out loud, 'Rock-n-Roll.'

He wandered around the Pigale district for a couple of hours, enjoying the sights and soaking up the atmosphere of this notorious area of elegant Paris. He stopped now and then for a drink at a bar or bistro, frequently declining, for the moment, the advances of the many ladies and boys of the night. He ate in a half decent Chinese restaurant and by eleven-thirty was ready to head over to *Les Plumes*, a burlesque nightclub, owned by an old acquaintance.

The taxi dropped him in front the gaudy entrance and, as he paid the fare, the driver gave a knowing wink and said, 'A good night for you, I think, monsieur.'

As Washington turned away, he said quietly, 'Fuck off,' then walked up the brightly illuminated steps and into *Les Plumes*.

The huge black man on the door bid him, 'Bonsoir, monsieur,' then gestured to the booth at the side of the hallway. The young woman at the desk smiled, and said, 'Trente euro, s'il vous plaît.'

Washington handed her the thirty euros and took the small ticket, which said, in French, English, and Russian, *First Drink Free.*

The midnight show was just starting as he made his way to the bar. He managed to get a stool at the end of the long counter and handed the barmaid his ticket. 'Beer, please.'

She returned with a small bottle of Heineken and placed it in front of him.

'Thanks. Is Madame Sofie in yet?'

The girl looked suspicious. 'Who wants to know?'

'Tell her it's the American.'

The girl looked him up and down for a second, then picked up a phone on the back counter. After the call, she turned away and carried on serving the customers.

Upstairs in her office, Madame Sofie studied the CCTV camera screen, then picked up the phone. A few minutes later another equally large black man came up to Washington and said, 'This way, monsieur.'

196

Rick took a swig from the bottle, then followed the man across the busy club and through a door marked PRIVEE. At the top of the stairs was a small landing with a red velvet chaise.

'Turn around,' said the big man.

After confiscating Rick's gun and knife the man said, 'Have a seat, monsieur,' then knocked on the door.

'Entrez.'

The man entered and closed the door behind him. A few seconds later the door opened again. 'Come in, monsieur.'

The person behind the desk must have weighed almost two hundred pounds and was one of the most unconvincing transvestites anyone was likely to see. Sitting on the desk was a beautiful Chinese girl. The big 'woman' patted her on the thigh and the girl leaned down and planted a lingering kiss on Madame Sofie's bright red lips. Washington smiled as the oriental and the black guy left. His gun and knife were in front of the woman.

As the door closed, he said, 'How ya doin, Charlie?'

In a deep Louisiana drawl, the woman said, 'The name's, Sofie. And who the hell are you?'

'Don't you recognise me, Charlie . . . Sofie?'

'Should I?'

'It's Greg. Greg Stoneham.'

'I don't know who you are sugar, but you ain't Greg Stoneham. You look nothing like him, which would still be difficult if you did, considering he died in Panama.'

Washington took a step forward and, in a single motion, the woman picked up the revolver cocked the hammer and pointed it at his chest. 'Easy now, sugar.'

Washington stopped and raised his left hand, palm open. 'Remember this, Sofie?'

She put on a pair of ornate spectacles, then waved him forward with her free hand. The revolver always pointed at his chest. He placed his hand flat on the desk, palm up. She adjusted the desk-lamp. With the gun still pointing at him, she looked at the hand. Then, with a long ruby-red nail, traced the **L**-shaped scar in the centre of his palm. She looked him in the eyes and said, 'Greg?'

He smiled. 'In the flesh.'

She lowered the gun and let the southern drawl ooze out, 'Why, Greg honey, you've had some work done.'

Chapter Fifty
'Dasvidanya'

Jack and Bogdan got back from Vauxhall Cross a little before 6pm. Mathew's driver had brought them back to East Monkton, this time without a police outrider, which upset the big Russian no end. The twins were delighted to have some time with their daddy and even more delighted to play with Daddy's big happy-faced friend.

At seven o'clock Svetlana, their nanny, gathered up the girls for bed, but not before everyone had been kissed and several hugs for Uncle Bogdan had been given. Nicole caught the smiles between Svetlana and Bogdan when the big man wished her 'Good night' as well.

After the girls had gone up, the three of them went out to the patio. The external lights came on illuminating the garden, trees and small lake.

'Is beautiful home here, boss,' said Bogdan.

'All Nikki's work, my friend.'

'Da, this I am sure.'

She kissed the big man on the cheek and said. 'I'll go and see how supper is doing.'

The two friends sat down, and Bogdan said, 'You are lucky man, boss. You have beautiful wife, beautiful family, beautiful home.'

'Yeah, buddy, I know.'

'So why you do the shit we do, Jack?'

It was rare for the Russian to call him by his name. Jack looked across at his friend and said, 'Why do you do it?'

'It doesn't not matter for me. I have no family like you. Only Grigory, my brother.'

'But you still haven't said why you do it, big man?'

'I guess it is who I am. This is why.'

Jack reached over and patted the big Russian's shoulder. 'Me too buddy. Me too.'

Nicole came back with a tray of drinks and said, 'What's going on here? You boys look very serious?'

Jack got up, took the tray, then kissed her. 'Just talking, darling. Just talking.'

'Supper will be ready in half an hour.'

Jack passed her a large glass of white wine and then handed Bogdan his beer. He picked up his Coke and said, 'To us. Nostrovia.'

The following morning breakfast was served on the patio. The girls were giving Svetlana a hard time over having to go to nursery, wishing to spend the day with Uncle Bogdan instead. Nicole's stern intervention convinced them it was time for nursery. That, and the promise from Daddy of special treats when they got home. More cuddles for Uncle Bogdan were given, then the twins reluctantly disappeared inside, quickly followed by a slightly red faced and harassed, Svetlana.

Jack and Nicole both asked Bogdan to stay for a few more days, but the big man was adamant he was heading home. 'You must be with family, boss. I go back to Moscow. Will see you again soon.'

Bogdan's flight was due to depart at 3pm, Jack said they should be there for midday, and would drive him to the airport. Much to the big Russian's delight, Nicole also insisted she came to see him off as well.

At the Departures Gate, Bogdan almost crushed Jack's still tender ribs, with his bear-hug. A decidedly gentler embrace was given to Nicole.

'Thank you for looking after him, Bogdan. Come back and see us very soon. Da?'

The big man's face beamed. 'Da, for sure I come back. I have nieces now. Da?'

She kissed his cheeks.

He turned to Jack and they shook hands. 'Dasvidanya, boss.'

'Dasvidanya, my friend. God bless.'

As the big Russian walked through the doors he turned, gave a huge smile, and flicked a casual salute.

Chapter Fifty One
'Welcome To England'

The chimes from the little church at the end of the street rang 6am. Rick Washington found it ironic, in a place as debauched as Pigale, the only sound in the morning came from a church. But then again, what better place to find souls to save.

The meeting with Madame Sofie had gone better than he'd hoped, and the twenty thousand dollars she'd asked for was less than he'd expected to pay, so he wasn't too upset when the contact she'd arranged showed up a few minutes late.

'You are the American?'

'Yeah. You are, Daniel?'

The man was in his mid-thirties, handsome and very fit-looking. He was dressed casually, but not expensively. 'Oui, monsieur, Daniel.'

'Okay, good. Let's go.'

They walked around the corner and along to the end of the street. The lights flashed on an old BMW.

The Frenchman said, 'Ici, monsieur.'

Washington climbed in and looked around. 'Is this thing gonna get us to the coast?'

The man winked and said, 'Don't let appearance fool you, American. This car will outrun most others.'

As the engine roared into life, Washington smiled.

At that time of the morning the traffic wasn't too bad, and they managed to get out of Montmartre, along Rue

Victor Hugo and across the Pont de Clichy, in less than thirty minutes. As they joined the A1 autoroute Daniel put his foot down. The big engine growled and the old BMW sped north at over 120 miles an hour. They entered the Calais Marina a few minutes before 9am.

Daniel parked the car and took a cold box and small holdall from the boot. Then they walked for about a hundred yards to one of the outer berths.

'This is it,' said the Frenchman.

Washington knew boats, and he was impressed with this one, a *Bayliner 285* cabin cruiser. New, one of these would cost over sixty-thousand dollars. This one looked new.

'Very nice. This is your boat, Daniel?'

The man shook his head as he untied the for'ard tether. 'This is Madame Sofie's.'

Washington stepped on board and said, 'What the hell does she wants a boat like this for?'

Daniel turned, and said, 'You think you are the first we take across the water, American?'

Washington smiled. 'Right . . . You can get quite a few illegals on this baby.'

The young man gestured towards two large plastic cylinders, hanging between the hull and the dock. 'Pull in the buffers, monsieur. We go now.'

The weather out in the Channel was reasonably calm, with a light swell and a warm wind from the south. Washington was surprised at the amount of shipping moving east and west in this narrow strip of sea.

From the cockpit Daniel shouted, 'You want some food, American?'

'Sure, what you got?'

'In the cold box. There is baguettes, fromage et jambon. Fruit. In the galley you can make coffee. There will be beers in fridge also.'

'This is almost First Class service.'

Over the roar of the engines Daniel shouted, 'What you say, monsieur? I don't hear.'

Washington shouted, 'I said, do you want anything?'

'Oui. Yes, a black coffee, s'il vous plaît.'

'Okay. One black coffee coming up, captain.'

A few minutes later, Washington appeared in the cockpit with coffees and sandwiches. 'How long to the coast?'

The Frenchman took the coffee and shook his head at the offer of a sandwich. 'Calais to Dover direct, is about one hour in this. But we shall go a little to the east of Dover, between Dover and Folkstone. There is a small bay where we can arrive,' he looked at his watch, 'we will be there by ten-thirty.'

Washington nodded as he bit into his baguette, then said, 'You will wait there for me to return?'

'No monsieur, it is too risky with the Anglais. I will drop you there and return to Calais. I will be back here tomorrow morning, same time, ten-thirty. Same place. This is okay?'

'Sure. I'll be there. You know the guy who's picking me up?'

'Oui, monsieur. He is my cousin. He will drive you from the coast to your destination. And return when you wish.'

Washington spilled his coffee, as the boat bounced against the waves. 'Shit.'

The Frenchman smiled at the accident. 'You okay, American?'

'Yeah. I'm okay.'

A little under an hour later the *Bayliner* slowed as it approached the Kent coast. Two hundred yards from shore Daniel dropped the anchor. 'Okay. Ici, American.'

'Can't we get closer?'

The Frenchman didn't answer. He went to the stern and lowered a small motor boat. A few minutes later, as he held the boat steady, he said, 'Okay, monsieur, Let's go.'

Washington climbed in, stumbling as the swell caught the small craft.

Daniel smiled. 'You okay?'

'I'm okay. Let's just get the fuck ashore.'

A few minutes later they pulled into a tiny cove. As the bow cut gently into the sand, a man appeared from what looked like a small cave. 'Daniel. Ça va?'

'Hi, Maurice. Ici, l'Americain.'

'Okay. Hello, monsieur. Vite. We go?'

As Washington jumped onto the beach, Maurice said. 'Welcome to England.'

Chapter Fifty Two
'The Butcher's Van'

The drive from the Kent coast to East Monkton had taken over three hours. It was a few minutes before 2pm when Maurice pulled into the lay-bay, a quarter of a mile from the gates of Jack Castle's home.

'Stay here until I get back.'

'Oui, monsieur. How long shall I wait?'

Washington turned and looked the man straight in the eyes. 'You stay right here until I return. You got me? You stay the fuck right here.'

'Okay, American. Be calm.'

Washington went to the boot and removed the Glock from his rucksack. He checked the magazine, then quickly fitted a small snub-nose silencer. He cocked the mechanism and slipped it into his inside pocket. The switch-blade was dropped into his back pocket and the Smith & Wesson into his waistband.

A car drove past and he turned his face away, so as not to be noticed. He closed the boot, then went to the driver's door. 'Be here when I get back.'

'Oui, monsieur. I will be here.'

As Washington walked slowly up the tree-lined lane, the Frenchman said, 'Asshole.'

The high gates were electrically controlled, with two sets of security cameras covering the front area. The ivy-covered wall looked to surround the property. From his concealed vantage point across the lane, Washington could see through the gates and up the drive to the impressive house.

He'd only been watching for a few minutes when a butcher's delivery truck approached and slowly turned into the entrance. In front of the gates he saw the driver's hand appear as he touched the intercom. He swiftly ran across the road and tried the van's back doors. Finding them locked he quickly moved away from the vehicle and into the bushes.

As the truck drove through the gates he made his move. Before they closed he was inside and again concealed behind a huge hydrangea, the chance of being caught on camera mitigated by the size of the butcher's van. If he had been seen, they would be coming for him. He waited. Nothing.

Almost twenty minutes later the delivery van came from the rear of the house and approached the gates. A few seconds later they swung open and he watched as the van drove off. He was about to move position, when the gates again swung silently open. He slipped back into the shadow of the bush as the big Jaguar passed him, Jack Castle at the wheel.

Chapter Fifty Three
'Stiff Upper Lip'

After leaving Heathrow Jack had taken Nicole to the *Blue Bell* at East Monkton, for lunch. The restaurant was one of their favourites and boasted two Michelin stars. Even though he hadn't booked, the Maître'd still managed to give them their favourite table overlooking the river. They both ate the excellent pâté, with a Cumberland sauce to die for. Nicole chose the salmon, Jack the veal. She drank a couple of glasses of white Zinfandel, Jack drank sparkling water. After being thanked by the Maître'd for the generous tip, they left the *Blue Bell* just after 3 o'clock.

As the Jaguar pulled up to the front of the house Nicole said, 'That was lovely, Zaikin. And very unexpected. If I'd known we were eating-out, I'd have got dressed.'

He leaned over and kissed her. 'You look wonderful, babe.'

From his concealed position near the gate, Rick Washington watched them walk into the hallway, then said quietly, 'Hello, again, Jack.'

It took almost ten minutes for him to move from the gate and up to the house. Each time looking for a secure and concealing position, always with his eyes on the building. As he moved to the side of the property he could see the conservatory and lake. 'Nice place, Jack,' he said under his breath, 'shame it's all gonna come down around your head.'

In the conservatory, Jack was scrolling through emails on his phone. Nicole and Svetlana played with the twins on the big rug.

Outside, Washington gently moved the ivy at the side of the glass wall and carefully peered into the conservatory. He steadied his breathing and then took the Smith & Wesson from his belt. He covered the ten feet to the open doors in a second.

The piercing noise of Svetlana's scream shocked everyone.

Jack jumped up at the sound and then turned to see his old adversary, the chrome revolver glinting in his hand. 'Take it easy, Jack. Don't try anything stupid,' he pointed to the twins, 'they'll get it first.'

Nicole moved to gather up her children. Washington yelled, 'Don't move. Stay still.'

Svetlana began to whimper.

'Shut the fuck up,' snarled Washington.

'Take it easy,' said Jack. 'It's me you want. Leave them out of this.'

'You shut the fuck up too. I'm in charge here. Who else is in the house?'

'No one,' said Nicole.

Washington smiled. 'Now don't be telling me any lies, honey. Or someone might get hurt.'

'There's a housekeeper in the kitchen. The gardener is on his day off,' said Jack

Washington pointed to the group on the rug. 'You. Go get her.'

Svetlana made to move, but Washington said, 'Not you. You go, Nicole. I know you'll come back, with your kids here.'

Nicole looked at Jack. He nodded, and she stood up.

'Oh, and don't think about calling the police, Mrs Castle. The first sound of a siren and they get it,' he nodded towards the twins, now in the arms of the sobbing nanny.

A few moments later Nicole and Maggie returned. 'Ah, the housekeeper. Thank you for joining us. Now, everyone sit down.'

Jack moved towards Nicole and took a seat. 'What is it you want?'

'I want everything you took from me, Jack. My three billion pounds, to start with.'

Jack shook his head slightly. 'I don't have that kind of money.'

'No, but daddy does. Doesn't he, Nicole?'

Washington saw the shadow and, as Brian swung the heavy spade, he ducked. The edge of the tool caught him a glancing blow on the shoulder. He fired. The bullet tore into Brian's upper chest, spinning him around and out through the open doors.

Jack threw himself at Washington, taking him down with a brutal tackle. 'Panic room,' he yelled.

The revolver, knocked from Rick's hand, slid across the floor and under a side table. The screaming women scooped up the twins and rushed from the conservatory.

Jack rolled over and punched the American hard in the ribs, another blow to the side of his head.

A knee into his groin made Jack yell out, the headbutt stunned him. He clung on to Washington, punching, kneeing, fighting to get the upper hand.

The American freed himself and scrambled to his feet, kicking at Jack, as he tried to pull the Glock from his inside pocket.

Jack rolled away, and then he too was on his feet, just as the second gun was drawn. Again, he charged. They stumbled, across the floor and into the hallway, a tangled mass of arms and legs, fighting, punching, gouging. No quarter given. Just pain for both, as they hit the marble floor.

In the panic room, Nicole held the children close, her eyes transfixed on the CCTV screen. Maggie was sitting in the corner, whimpering, clearly in a state of shock. Svetlana stood next to the children, cursing the attacker in Russian, as the bloody fight unfolded on the tiny monitor.

Jack felt his already bruised ribs break, as the American delivered a vicious elbow hard into his chest, driving the oxygen from his lungs. He yelled in agony, as Washington rammed the switch-blade deep into his thigh.

With the last of his strength, he yanked out the knife and slashed at the American's back.

Washington screamed, as the razor sharp blade cut deep into his flesh. He tried to stand but slipped on the crimson pool of Jack's blood.

211

Then he was on his feet. Heart pounding. Breath hissing from his bloodied mouth. The Glock in his hand.

They looked at each other, both gasping for breath. Saying nothing.

At last Washington spoke. 'Jesus Christ, Jack, you're one tough mother-fucker.'

Jack sat up, holding the bloody wound in his thigh. He grinned, and said, 'You too.'

'So, this is it eh, Mr Castle?'

Jack wiped the blood from his eyes, and said, 'The police will be here any minute. The alarm in the panic room will bring them.'

Washington smiled for a second, then his eyes narrowed, and the smile was gone. 'I don't think so, Jack. The nearest police station is at Great Monkton, and that's at least fifteen minutes' drive away. And even if they have been told of the alarm, they don't have an armed unit there,' he grinned, 'I don't suppose there's much call for gun-toting cops in Berkshire.'

'They'll still be here.'

'Maybe, but that's not gonna help you, Jack. You Brits are not gonna send your famous bobbies into a gunfight unarmed. No . . . the soonest a tactical team could get here would be thirty-five, maybe forty minutes from London, and that's by chopper. You and your family will all be dead, and this house burning to the ground, by then.'

Jack's mind was racing, his thoughts only of his family. *The Panic-Room was secure, fully insulated, self-contained air for twelve hours. A fire wouldn't harm them. My girls will survive.* 'Get on with it then. Just do me a favour and stop fuckin talking.'

'Ahh . . . there it is, the British stiff upper lip. Stoic to the end. Well done, Jack.'

'Fuck you.'

'Yes, quite.' Washington raised the gun and said, 'I'd toyed with the idea of not killing you immediately. Taking my time. Enjoying it. But I think under the circumstances, time is of the essence, and unfortunately, I need to go. So, its gonna have to be quick.' The American smiled as he took aim. 'Bye, Jackie boy.'

The crack of the gunshot was much louder than Jack expected from the silenced weapon. Blood splattered his face and chest, the cloying liquid in his eyes and mouth. For a second he was blinded . . . then, he looked up at Washington.

The American's smile had turned into a grimacing death rictus, his forehead blown open.

Then, like an old chimney being brought down in slow motion, Rick Washington, former CIA agent, contract terrorist and mass murderer, finally fell.

For several seconds Jack lay still. The lifeless body pinned him to the floor. He sucked in a lung-full of air, then heaved Washington's carcass off.

Nicole stood a few yards away, arms outstretched, hands together in the classic shooter's stance, the chrome Smith & Wesson still pointing to where Washington had stood. A thin wisp of blue smoke drifted from the gun's muzzle and floated up the stair-well.

Groaning, Jack pulled himself up and limped slowly towards her. The beautiful face pale, tears trickled slowly down her cheeks.

'Nicole . . . It's me, darling. It's Jack. Give me the gun.' He slowly moved to her side and gently eased the weapon from her now trembling hands. 'Nicole,' he said softly, 'everything's alright, my darling. You're safe. Our girls are safe. I'm safe.'

She slowly turned to him and looked up at his blood spattered face. 'Jack?'

He wrapped his arms around her and held her to his chest. 'Yes, it's me, Nikki. It's me.'

Epilogue

A couple of days later . . .

In *The Chiltern Clinic,* one of the most exclusive private hospitals in Berkshire, Maggie Walker sat at her husband's bedside. 'How're you feeling today, love?'

'Getting better, Mags. Don't worry, old love.'

'I was thinking, Brian. Maybe it's time to retire?'

As he grinned, he held his hand to the heavy dressing on his chest. 'And what, miss out on all this fun?'

In the upstairs office of *Les Plumes,* Madame Sofie looked at the pile of cash in front of her.

'How much did you say, Daniel?'

'Almost four-hundred thousand, Madame.'

'From behind the wardrobe?'

'Oui, Madame.'

She smiled then counted out fifty-thousand. She slid the pile across her desk to the handsome Frenchman, blew him a kiss and said, 'That's for you, sugar.'

Sir Anthony Grainger's funeral was attended by over three hundred of the great-and-the-good, including the Prime Minister and her Cabinet. As his coffin was carried from the Church, Gary, his former Special Branch bodyguard, said to himself, *I told you I should have come with you, Sir Anthony.*

In Wales, a couple of fell walkers sat down to rest by a burnt-out farmhouse. The day was clear, and they could see all the way to the Irish Sea. After finishing their energy drinks, they were about to leave, when a peregrine falcon swooped down and perched on the carcass of the farmhouse.

'Look at that,' said one.

'Yeah, what a beautiful bird.'

Their voices startled the hunter and it took flight. For several seconds they watched the elegant creature soar higher and higher, then disappear into the clear blue sky.

A couple of weeks later . . .

Two blocks from Red Square, Bogdan Markov walked out of the *Moskva-Siti Bank* with a huge grin on his face. His brother Grigory waited in the big Mercedes.

As his brother climbed in, Grigory said, 'Okay?'

Bogdan nodded, took a sheet of paper from his inside pocket, and handed it to Grigory.

Grigory's mouth fell open. 'Three million sterling?'

'Da,' said Bogdan,' three million sterling.'

They both laughed.

A courier arrived at the big house in East Monkton. At the door he handed Jack a large envelope, embossed with the seal of the British Government. Inside was a hand written letter from the Prime Minister, which read . . .

Dear Jack.

I cannot express my gratitude enough, for your key role in the successful outcome of the recent enterprise. I am

216

told you have sustained several injuries, from which I hope you will soon be fully recovered.

I would also like to extend an invitation to you and your wife, to spend the weekend with us at Chequers, once you are fully able.

Finally, and I am delighted to advise, you will receive the Order of the British Empire, in the New Year. We would however appreciate your discretion, until your award is advised formally in the usual manner.

Please extend my best wishes to your lady wife and thank you once again.

RS

A couple of months later . . .

In the Great Hall of the Castello San Lorenzo, a short ceremony was coming to a close. Thirteen chairs were arranged in a circle, all save one, were occupied. In the centre, stood a man dressed in evening wear. Over his clothes he wore a white linen tabard, emblazoned with a red cruciform cross. In one hand he held an old leather bound bible, in the other, an ornate dagger.

The man was finishing his address. 'On my honour, I am bound by these values and should I betray this society, then let me be stripped of my raiment. Let my tongue be torn from my mouth. Let this dagger pierce my heart, and my remains be cast on the waters as carrion . . . Semper Fidelis.'

Later, an elegantly dressed woman spoke to the man. 'Welcome to the Templari Incrementum, Dimitri.'

The man raised his glass. 'Thank you, Contessa.'

The End, but . . .

Jack Castle will be back . . .